INVISIBLE

FIENDS

MR MUMBLES

BARRY HUTCHISON

INVISIBLE

FIENDS

MR MUMBLES

First published in paperback in Great Britain by
HarperCollins *Children's Books* 2010

HarperCollins *Children's Books* is a division of HarperCollins*Publishers* Ltd
77-85 Fulham Palace Road, Hammersmith, London W6 8JB

Visit us on the web at www.harpercollins.co.uk
Visit Barry at www.barryhutchison.com

Text copyright © Barry Hutchison 2009

ISBN 978-0-00-731515-4

Printed and bound in England by Clays Ltd, St Ives plc

To Fiona. My best friend (real, not imagined).

Will you marry me?

PROLOGUE

What had I expected to see? I wasn't sure. An empty street. One or two late-night wanderers, maybe.

But not this. Never this.

There were hundreds of them. *Thousands*. They scuttled and scurried through the darkness, swarming over the village like an infection; relentless and unstoppable.

I leaned closer to the window and looked down at the front of the hospital. One of the larger creatures was tearing through the fence, its claws slicing through the wrought-iron bars as if they were cardboard. My breath fogged the glass and the monster vanished behind a cloud of condensation. By the time the pane cleared the *thing* would be inside the hospital. It would be up the stairs in moments. Everyone in here was as good as dead.

The distant thunder of gunfire ricocheted from somewhere near the village centre. A scream followed – short and sharp, then suddenly silenced. There were no more gunshots after that, just the triumphant roar of something sickening and grotesque.

I heard Ameena take a step closer behind me. I didn't need to look at her reflection in the window to know how terrified she was. The crack in her voice said it all.

'It's the same everywhere,' she whispered.

I nodded, slowly. 'The town as well?'

She hesitated long enough for me to realise what she meant. I turned away from the devastation outside. 'Wait... You really mean *everywhere*, don't you?'

Her only reply was a single nod of her head.

'*Liar!*' I snapped. It couldn't be true. This couldn't be happening.

She stooped and picked up the TV remote from the day-room coffee table. It shook in her hand as she held it out to me.

'See for yourself.'

Hesitantly, I took the remote. 'What channel?'

She glanced at the ceiling, steadying her voice. 'Any of them.'

The old television set gave a faint *clunk* as I switched it on. In a few seconds, an all-too-familiar scene appeared.

Hundreds of the creatures. Cars and buildings ablaze. People screaming. People running. People *dying*.

Hell on Earth.

'That's New York,' she said.

Click. Another channel, but the footage was almost identical.

'London.'

Click.

'I'm... I'm not sure. Somewhere in Japan. Tokyo, maybe?'

It could have been Tokyo, but then again it could have been anywhere. I clicked through half a dozen more channels, but the images were always the same.

'It happened,' I gasped. 'It actually happened.'

I turned back to the window and gazed out. The clouds above the next town were tinged with orange and red. It was already burning. They were destroying everything, just like *he'd* told me they would.

This was it.

The world was ending.

Armageddon.

And it was all my fault.

THIRTY-FOUR DAYS EARLIER...

Chapter One

JINGLE HELL

If Nan had made the joke about the frosted glass once, she'd made it a hundred times. It wasn't even very funny the first time round.

'Look, Kyle,' she'd say between tracks of the cheesy Christmas hits CD she was inflicting on me, 'the glass in the windows is more frosted up than the frosted glass in the door!'

The first few times I laughed. The next few I smiled and nodded. By the seventh time I'd taken to ignoring her completely. It was the only way she was going to learn.

Don't get me wrong, it's not like I don't like my nan. She's actually pretty cool most of the time. For a seventy-four-year-old with two plastic hips, anyway. It's just that her mind plays tricks on her sometimes.

Up until I was about six or seven, Nan used to stay here in the house with us. It was Nan, Mum and me, all living together and getting along fine.

Then one day Nan forgot her name. It just popped right out of her head one morning, and she had to ask Mum what it was. The whole thing seemed hilarious to me at the time, though Nan and Mum didn't see the funny side.

Everything was OK again for a while, then Nan started to get more and more confused. She'd wake up in the night and not know where she was. Some days she'd believe she was a little girl again, dodging the bombs in the Second World War.

One time she thought I'd vanished. For three whole days she couldn't see or hear me, even when I was standing right in front of her, waving my arms and shouting. It freaked Mum out. After that, the doctor said it was best if she didn't live with us any more.

The home Mum found for her seemed quite nice. Everyone there was friendly, and Nan seemed happy enough. She still spends every Christmas Day with us, but I don't get to see her much apart from that. The doctor says she's getting more and more confused with every day that passes, so she's pretty much confined to the home all year round. She doesn't seem to mind.

Her 'confusion' was why she kept repeating the joke about the frosted glass over and over. Well, that and the fact she'd had four sherries in forty minutes.

When Nan wasn't making wisecracks about the temperature she was grinning like a maniac, and watching me play with the action figures she'd given me. Every year I try to explain that I haven't played with action figures since I was five. Every year she buys me more.

Last year it was Power Rangers. The year before that it was Spider-Man. The years before that? I can't remember. I had no idea who this year's merry band of misfits were, either. One looked like a cat dressed as a cowboy. If I kind of closed one eye and tilted my head to the side another one looked like a monkey in a dress. A bit.

I did my best to look excited for Nan's sake, and smacked

them against each other a few times as if they were fighting. Even now, with all the crazy stuff I've seen in the past few hours, I can't think of many reasons why a cowboy cat would be fighting a monkey in a dress. It seemed to make Nan happy, though, so I kept it up until she started snoring her head off in front of the fire.

With Nan asleep I was free to go and check out the smell that had been wafting in from the kitchen for the last twenty minutes. Mum was making Christmas lunch for the three of us, and I could hardly wait.

Usually Mum's cooking was something to be avoided. Feared, even. For a woman who could burn a boiled egg, though, she somehow always managed to make a mean turkey with all the trimmings come December 25th. It was her own kind of Christmas magic. Not as spectacular as flying around the world in one night, but impressive all the same. Such a gift, of course, didn't come without a price...

'Kyle Alexander, touch those sausages and I'll break your fingers!' Mum snapped. I hadn't even noticed the plate of half-sized bangers cooling on a wire rack next to the cooker

until then, but suddenly I wanted them more than anything else in the world. 'I mean it,' she scolded, stepping back to avoid the heat as she yanked open the oven door and slung in a tray of potatoes. 'I need them. If you're hungry have a mince pie.'

'I'm not hungry,' I shrugged, and I wasn't. I just wanted a little sausage. The look on Mum's face told me if I took one I'd be signing my death warrant, so I slowly stepped away, keeping my hands in clear view at all times. For 364 days of the year Mum is pretty easy-going, but mess with her when she's making Christmas dinner and you're opening the door to a world of pain.

She swept past me and tore open a drawer. I could hear her muttering to herself as she rummaged around, getting more and more annoyed as she realised that whatever she was looking for wasn't where she thought it was.

'Need a hand?' I asked. I didn't know the first thing about cooking, but thought I'd offer anyway.

'Have you seen the – *Aha*!' Like a tiger pouncing on its prey, Mum bounded across the kitchen and snatched up two complicated-looking kitchen utensils. At least I guessed that was what they were. They might have been instruments of torture for all I knew. In the mood she was in she'd probably use them too.

I knew it wasn't the right time to ask the question. Sometimes it seems like it's never the right time to ask the question. I always ask it anyway. I can't help it. It just slips out.

'Any word from Dad?'

Mum sighed and slammed the utensils down on the kitchen counter. She hung her head, her back towards me, saying nothing. The only sounds were the howling of the wind outside and the steady rattling of Nan snoring in the living room.

'Not this again,' breathed Mum. Her voice wasn't angry like I'd expected it to be. It just sounded tired. She turned to face me and I could see that the lines of her face were drawn with sadness. 'No, Kyle,' she said, 'there's been no word from Dad. Just like there was no word from him last year, or any year before that.'

I don't know why I think about my dad so much, what with me never having met him. I can't help that either. I wonder every day what he's like. Do I look like him? Do we sound the same? I don't even know his name.

'Maybe he'll phone,' I said, thinking it out loud more than anything else. I jumped as a plate smashed on the kitchen floor.

'No, he won't phone!' Mum cried. That had done it, she was properly angry now. 'He'll never phone! He doesn't care about us! When are you going to accept that?'

I felt tears spring to my eyes, as much for Mum as for myself. Why did I always push her like this? I should have let it go then, but I couldn't.

'He does care,' I shouted, my voice sounding much bolder than I was feeling. 'He'll come back one day, you'll see.'

'Oh, and what then?' Mum demanded, throwing her hands up into the air. 'You'll go off with him and live happily ever after, will you?'

From the way she said it I knew Mum was only looking for reassurance. She just wanted to know that I loved her and that I wouldn't choose someone over her who'd walked out before I was even born. I knew that was what she needed to hear, so I don't know why I said what I did.

'Maybe I will.'

She stared at me for a few long moments, her face a melting pot of betrayal and shock. I bit my lip, wishing I could take the words back. She took a steadying breath and patted down a crease on the front of her *World's Best Mum* apron.

'I think you should go to your room, Kyle,' she said. Her voice was flat and controlled. Suddenly the kitchen felt as frosty as the glass in the window frame.

'But what about dinner?' I protested. 'It's Christmas dinner!'

'Your room,' she repeated. 'Now.'

Usually I like lying on top of my bed. It's a comfy place to come and read, or just to think. I hoped I might get a games console for Christmas, so I could play it up in my room, but no such luck. I have a TV, but it's old and falling apart. On the rare times it actually picks up a channel, the picture is usually too snowy to watch. Still, I have my books and comics, and can normally pass a few hours with those.

Apart from the dodgy TV and the lack of games consoles, the only real downside to my room is the view from my window. Mum has a great view from hers. Our terrace is right up on top of a hill, so from Mum's room you can look out over the whole village. OK, so the village itself doesn't look all that impressive, but on clear nights you can make out all the lights of the next town, twinkling away happily in the distance.

It's a four- or five-mile trek to town, but it's worth it. If you're looking for decent shops, or a cinema, or anything at all, you'll find it in town. Even my school is there, which means a twenty-minute bus journey there and back every day during term time.

Our village has nothing very exciting in it. We've got houses, a couple of churches and a tiny supermarket whose shelves are always half empty.

Oh, and there's a police station. A lot of the time it's

unmanned, but sometimes – maybe when they need a rest, or something – one of the officers from the town comes over there for the day. They usually spend the whole time sitting with their feet up because – to be honest – there's not a lot happens in our village.

Beyond the town lie the mountains. They look brilliant at this time of year – the snow is almost right down to the bottom – and if I get my binoculars out I can sometimes see some of the kids from school sledging on the lower slopes. It looks like fun. Maybe one day I'll ask them if I can come. Then again, they'll probably only say 'no', so maybe I won't bother.

So, yeah, anyway, it's a good view from Mum's room. Mine isn't so great. In fact it's fair to say that my view gives me the willies. You see, unluckily for me, my bedroom faces straight on to the creepy abandoned house next door. The Keller House.

When I was eight or nine I kept asking Mum why we couldn't just move into the house. It's much bigger than ours, with a massive garden. It also has a room built on to the side with a private pool, but I hate water, so I wasn't too bothered about that. I just liked the idea of having a gigantic bedroom.

But that was before I heard the stories. Before I found out all about the Keller House. After that, I didn't want to go near the place. No one did.

So, as I was saying, I usually liked lazing on my bed, but lying there playing the conversation with Mum over and over in my head, it was the most uncomfortable place in the world.

I shouldn't have said the stuff I did, I knew that. The fact was, though, I *did* want to know about my dad. Mum never told me anything other than that he disappeared the day she told him she was pregnant with me.

Maybe she was right. Maybe he really didn't want anything to do with me. He'd made no effort to get in touch my whole life, after all. Still, something kept telling me I should keep asking, and it seemed as if I was powerless to fight the urge.

Up above me a shiny plastic Santa swung gently backwards and forwards on an invisible breeze. My eyes tick-tocked left and right, following his jolly pendulum sway. On each upward swing the glow from my light glinted off his oval eyes, making them appear glistening and alive.

Then, without warning, the overhead light went dim. For a moment it flicked and flickered, sending distorted Santa shadows scurrying up the wall. The wind shook the window, rattling it in its wooden frame. The bedroom door creaked loudly as a draft slowly pushed it closed.

With a distant *fzzzt* the room was plunged into almost total blackness. The faint, grey December daylight that seeped into the room barely made a dent in the dark.

Suddenly, over the howling of the gales outside, I heard a sharp scraping sound. It was slow at first, almost methodical. Quickly, though, it picked up pace, until a frantic, desperate scratching ripped through the gloom.

There was a crazed urgency to the sound which froze me to my core. I lay still, unable to do anything but listen to the racket. It bounced off every wall, as if it were coming at me from every direction at once, making it almost impossible for me to pinpoint the source.

It took me several seconds, but eventually I realised where the horrible scratching was coming from: the ceiling above my bed. The blood in my veins ran as cold as ice.

There was something in the attic.

And it was trying to claw its way through.

Chapter Two

A FORGOTTEN FRIEND

I don't remember jumping off my bed but I must've done, because the next thing I knew I was standing in the middle of the room, listening to the scraping above me. Whatever was up there was ripping furiously at the attic floor, scratching and clawing its way through the wood.

Outside, the wind screeched and howled and hurled itself against the glass, as if it too was trying to force its way into my bedroom. The darkness seemed to close in. It wrapped around me like an icy shroud, squeezing the air from my lungs and making my heart thud faster and faster and faster.

My head went light and I felt the carpet turn to quicksand below me, sucking me down. I dropped to my knees, choking and struggling to breathe, as the world began to spin.

The sound of that scratching grew louder and louder until it was the only thing I could hear. I covered my ears, desperately trying to block it out, but still it grew louder until I was sure my head was going to explode with it.

With a faint *clunk* the room was filled with light, and the scratching came to an abrupt stop.

'Nothing to worry about, just a fuse,' I heard Mum shout. 'You OK?'

I opened my mouth to answer, but barely a whimper came out. The carpet was rough against my cheek, and I realised I was lying curled up on the floor, my knees almost to my chest. My arms shook as I tried to push myself into a sitting position.

'Kyle, what's wrong?' Mum asked, her voice urgent and panicked as she pushed open my door. My head splitting with a ferocious ache, I turned and looked up at her. She knelt by my side and stroked my face with the back of her hand, wiping away tears I hadn't even felt fall. 'What happened?' she asked, softly.

'The attic,' I managed to hiss. 'I heard something in the attic. Scratching.'

Mum leaned back on her heels, her eyes and mouth – just for a moment – three little circles of surprise. She gave an almost invisible shake of her head and smiled.

'It was just your mind playing tricks on you,' she assured me.

'What? No it wasn't!' I insisted, annoyed that she'd think I'd let my imagination run away with me like that. 'I heard something scratching up there!'

'You know what I think?' she smiled. 'I think you got a scare when the lights went out and maybe had a little panic attack.'

'I did not!'

'Hard to breathe,' said Mum, listing off the symptoms, 'wobbly legs, feel like the room's closing in on you...'

Reluctant as I was to admit it, it would help explain why I'd reacted the way I had. I'd never felt that scared before, and all because of what? A scraping noise? Idiot.

'OK,' I reluctantly confessed, 'maybe it was.' Mum flashed me a sympathetic smile and rustled my hair. 'You seem to know a lot about them,' I said. 'Do you get them?'

'Me? No,' said Mum, shaking her head. 'But your da—'

She stopped, biting her lip just as I had done in the kitchen. She'd almost let something slip about my dad.

'But my dad did,' I guessed. 'That's what you were going to say, wasn't it? You were going to tell me my dad used to have panic attacks.'

'No, I wasn't,' Mum replied. She had her defences back up and was getting to her feet. 'I was going to say you're darn lucky you don't get them more often.'

She was lying, I could tell, but she was making for the door now, and more than anything I didn't want to be left alone in this room.

'Mum!' I spluttered. She stopped in the doorway, hesitated, then turned back to me. I should have told her I was sorry for our argument in the kitchen, but when I opened my mouth all that came out was: 'I really did hear something in the attic.'

Mum looked at me for a long time, her eyes scanning my face. Eventually, she shrugged and smiled a thin-lipped smile.

'Well, then. Let's check it out.'

*

A chill breeze rolled down through the hole in the ceiling as Mum slid back the lock and let the wooden hatch swing open. Stale, years-old air filled my nostrils, forcing me to take a step back. The smell reminded me of the day room in the home Nan stays in. Somewhere in the shadows, the hot water boiler hissed quietly, making it sound as if the loft itself was breathing.

The beam of Mum's torch cut through the darkness of the attic, projecting a misshapen circle of light on to the bare wooden planks of the roof. Shoulder to shoulder we stood on our tiptoes, peering into the gloom.

'See anything?' I asked, trying to disguise the shake in my voice.

'Nothing from here,' Mum replied. Her voice sounded confident – a little amused, even. I felt a hot flush of embarrassment sweep up from my neck. I was acting like a scared kid, and she knew it. 'I'll pull the ladder down and we can have a proper look,' she said, passing me the torch.

She reached carefully up through the hatch and felt

around for the edge of the wooden steps. My breath caught at the back of my throat, as Mum suddenly let out a sharp cry of fright. As one, we staggered backwards away from the hole, until our backs were flat against the wall. Hands shaking, I directed the torch's beam up into the attic once again, and almost screamed. Just inside the hatch a pair of piercing eyes glowed brightly in the trembling torchlight.

'M-Mum,' I began, not knowing where the rest of the sentence was going. I was gripping her arm tightly, too terrified to move.

Then, with a faint *squeak*, the eyes turned and darted off into the darkness of the roof space. For a moment we heard the mouse's claws scrape against the wooden floor as it fled in panic.

I blushed for the second time in as many minutes, as Mum looked down at me. Quickly, I let go of her arm, trying to pretend I hadn't been afraid. She saw right through it, though, and I heard her let out a giggle. Before I knew it I was giggling along with her. We stood there together for a while, laughing out of sheer relief, until our sides ached and tears ran down our cheeks.

'You hungry?' she asked, when we'd both calmed down a bit.

'Depends. Are we allowed to eat the little sausages yet?'

'Come on,' she grinned, 'let's go have dinner.' Arm in arm we walked down the stairs, and every time our eyes met laughter filled the air.

Nan watched me impatiently as I cut her turkey into bite-sized chunks. She was proud of the fact she still had her own teeth, and mentioned it to anyone who'd listen. What she failed to go on to say was that they were now so blunt they could barely get through custard. Her arthritis was playing up with the cold, so I'd ended up on slice-and-dice duties.

She'd chuckled when me and Mum had told her the mouse story, but it didn't amuse her as much as it had us. I suppose you really had to be there.

'At least it wasn't that other fella,' she said, as I cut and peeled the skin off her little sausages. She didn't eat the skin, it gave her wind. Nan didn't actually mind too much, but Mum and me had insisted we remove them.

'What other fella?' I asked, only half listening. I was thinking about my own dinner, which would be getting cold.

'Oh, you remember,' she clucked, knocking back another glug of sherry, 'that friend of yours. Wassisname? Used to live in the loft, you said.'

I heard Mum's fork screech against her plate. She gave a cough which clearly meant 'shut up', but either Nan didn't notice, or she was too tipsy to care.

'Mr Mumbles,' she announced, triumphantly. 'That was him! Your invisible friend.' She smiled at the memory. 'Bless.'

Something tingled deep within my brain, and then was gone. I glanced over at Mum, but she had her head down, her eyes focused on her plate.

'I didn't have an invisible friend,' I frowned. 'Did I, Mum?'

'For a little while,' Mum said, not looking up from her dinner. 'It was a long time ago. You stopped talking about him years back.'

I finished cutting up Nan's meat and gave her back her

knife and fork. She was already shovelling turkey into her mouth by the time I made it round to my side of the table.

Me and Mum had taken the table through to the living room so we could eat in front of the fire. Normally we just ate on our laps, but Christmas dinner was special.

Still wracking my brains, I lowered myself back on to my chair and popped a chunk of carrot in my mouth. It tasted better than carrot had any right to taste. How did Mum do it?

'I don't remember,' I shrugged, at last.

'You were only four or five,' Mum explained. 'A long time ago. It's no surprise you've forgotten.'

'Used to talk about him all the time,' said Nan, her mouth half full of mashed potato. 'Mr Mumbles this, it was. Mr Mumbles that.'

'Leave it, Mum,' my mum said. 'He doesn't remember, let's leave it at that.'

'He used to live in the loft, you said,' Nan continued, completely ignoring her. 'You used to say he'd knock on your bedroom window when he wanted to play. Remember, Fiona?'

Mum glared at her. 'Leave it, I said.'

'Knock, knock!'

'Mum! *Enough!*'

Nan pulled a face, and silence fell over the table. I mopped up some gravy with a slice of turkey and slipped it in my mouth. Something stirred at the back of my mind.

'Wait,' I said. 'Was there… did he have a hat?'

'Let's just forget it, Kyle,' Mum urged.

'There's something… I think I remember something about a hat.'

'*I said forget it!*' Mum snapped. She slammed her hand down on the table, making the salt and pepper cellars leap into the air.

'O-OK,' I muttered, too shocked to argue. Mum's knife and fork were trembling in her hands as she got stuck back into her turkey. Something about me having an imaginary friend had clearly upset her.

But why?

'Bye, Nan,' I smiled, kissing her on her wrinkled cheek. We were exactly the same size these days. She was shrinking as fast as I was growing, and we were now passing each other as our heights headed in opposite directions.

'What?' She looked at me, her eyes narrowed, her voice a suspicious hiss.

'Um... I just said 'bye'.'

'Who are you?' she demanded, fiercely. 'I don't know you. Where's Albert? What have you done with my Albert?'

Nan spoke about Albert lots when she was confused. Not even Mum knew who he was. The best she could figure out was that Albert must have been some childhood friend of Nan's, but there was no way of knowing for sure. When Nan was her normal self she had no idea who Albert was, either.

'Come on,' said Mum, gently, as she guided Nan out of the house and into the chill darkness of the December night. 'Time we were getting you back.'

'Back where? What are you doing?' Nan spat, struggling against Mum's grip. 'Albert! *Albert!*'

No matter how many times I'd seen Nan have one of her episodes, it still shook me up. Mum's face was grey, her lips pursed together, as she tried to guide her mother towards the car.

'Come on, Mum,' she urged, forcing a smile.

'Right you are, love,' Nan replied. The smile was back on her face. Her eyes had their old twinkle again. As quickly as it had come on, the confusion had passed. She turned to me and gave a little wave. 'Merry Christmas, sweetheart,' she beamed.

'Merry Christmas, Nan.'

'Oh, and Kyle, be careful,' she said. 'There's a storm coming.'

'I think it's passed,' I said, gently. The winds had been howling and the rain battering down for days in the lead up to Christmas, but now it was calm – cold and frosty, but calm.

'Oh, but they come back,' warned Nan. Her face had taken on a strange, sombre expression. 'They always come back.'

'OK,' I said, humouring her. 'Bye.'

She gave me a nod and turned to Mum. 'Can I bring the sherry?'

'I think you've had quite enough for now,' Mum said, releasing her grip on Nan's arm. 'The nurses are going to kill me when they see the state of you!'

Nan cackled and gave me a theatrical wink. Without a word she turned and wandered off , swaying slightly in the chill evening gloom.

'Least it didn't last long this time. She's been pretty good, considering,' Mum whispered to me. 'You sure you'll be OK on your own? You can always come with us.'

'I'll be fine.'

'OK, well, I shouldn't be more than an hour. I'll just get her in and let the nurses put her to bed.'

'Can't she just stay here?' I asked.

'The doctors don't like it if she's gone overnight,' Mum said. I could tell from her face she felt bad about it. 'We'll play a board game or something when I get back, OK?'

'OK, but really, there's no rush,' I assured her. 'I'll be fine here on my own.'

She leaned forward and kissed me on the forehead. She was halfway to the gate when a thought struck her.

'Do me a favour while I'm out, will you?'

'Sure,' I nodded.

'There's a mousetrap in the cupboard under the sink. Stick it in the attic for me?'

Despite the tingling terror which crept over me, I nodded. I stood there, long after the door was closed, telling myself there was nothing to worry about. Telling myself not to be so stupid. After all, the scratching I'd heard was just a harmless little mouse.

Wasn't it?

Chapter Three

GHOSTS OF THE PAST

My breath formed faint clouds in the musty air as I pulled myself up into the confines of the attic. My fingers left ten little ovals in the thin covering of dust on the ladder, and I studied them for a few moments, pretending to myself they were the most interesting things in the world. Truth be told, I was just delaying the moment I'd have to step further into the loft.

The torch I carried was near powerless against the sheer depth of the darkness, like trying to slay a dragon with a teaspoon. The beam wobbled and shook in my hand, sending twisted shadows stretching across the planks and beams.

'There's nothing here,' I whispered, trying to reassure myself. 'There's nothing here except me and a mouse.'

I let the torch's beam fall on to the floor as I looked around for somewhere to put the mousetrap. It was tempting to just drop the thing and run, but the instructions had said to set it near a wall, and the last thing I wanted was to have to come back up and do all this over again.

The floorboards creaked in protest as I shuffled forwards, fixing my eyes on the point the roof met the floor. I would set the trap and then get out of there as quickly as I could. I'd be back downstairs in less than a minute. I just had to keep my nerve until then. Sixty seconds of bravery, that was all.

I set the torch on top of a dusty cardboard box and fumbled with the trap. Stupidly I'd left the instructions in the kitchen, thinking it would just be a case of pulling back a spring and sticking a bit of cheese on to a spike. That's how they always work in cartoons, anyway.

Around three minutes later, with my heart still thudding against the inside of my chest, I finally figured out how the trap operated. Hurriedly, I sat it down on the floorboards and gently pushed it against the wall, being careful not to bring it snapping down on my fingers. Since it didn't seem to be required, I decided just to eat the little cube of cheese I'd brought up with me.

Mission accomplished, I leapt to my feet. My head thumped against a thick roof beam and I cried out in pain. I rubbed the back of my skull and looked at my hands. They were clean, so I wasn't bleeding. That didn't stop it hurting, though.

I reached down to pick up the torch, then stopped. A piece of paper lay next to it on top of the box. I hadn't noticed it there when I'd walked over, but there it was, large as life. As I picked it up, the sheet felt oddly warm against my fingertips.

Angling the paper into the torchlight, I studied the crudely drawn crayon picture. Thick bands of black and brown covered most of the page, stretching down from the top of the paper to the bottom. Here and there the lines were broken by clumsy sketches of spiders skulking in their webs.

Two figures stood at opposite ends of the page. On the right-hand side a stick figure of a boy had been drawn, a tiny bow clutched in his pudgy round hands. Leading up and to the left were a dozen or so arrows, each with a bright red rubber suction cup stuck on to the end. They were all arching through the air in the direction of the other figure – a darkly dressed man.

My eyes followed the arrow trail and fell on the only other patch of red on the page. A demented fountain of blood sprayed out from the man's chest, where an arrow had embedded itself. His mouth – not surprisingly given the circumstances – was pulled into an upside down letter U. Clearly he was not happy with this turn of events.

I stared closely at this larger figure. There was something about him which intrigued me. He seemed to be drawn in a different style. He was darker, bolder, as if the crayons had been pressed harder against the page. He was also dressed strangely, with a long grey overcoat pulled up to his ears, and a black hat pulled down almost to meet it.

The image stirred some long dormant memories. That hat. That coat. It was all familiar but unfamiliar at the same time, like the memory of a dream I couldn't hold on to. Was this my imaginary friend?

Absent-mindedly, my gaze shifted across the page. There was something familiar about those vertical stripes, too. Were they bars? No, they were too thick for that. They looked solid, though. Solid; brown; evenly spaced. I'd seen them somewhere recently, but where?

The realisation hit me like an electric shock. I spun to face the attic wall. The lines in the picture weren't bars. They were beams. Wooden roof beams, like the kind I was standing next to. The picture was of right here in the attic!

A movement off to my left broke my concentration and I gasped with fright. Dropping the page I staggered back, knocking the box with my leg. My stomach lurched as the beam of the torch swung down. I grabbed for it too late. As the torch bulb smashed the attic was plunged into absolute darkness.

'Wh-who's there?' I stammered. With the light gone I couldn't even see the clouds of breath in front of my face any more. I held my breath and listened, but the only reply was the hissing and bubbling of the hot water boiler.

I tried to tell myself I'd imagined it, but if truth be told I don't have that good an imagination. Something had moved. Something was there in the attic with me, and unless mice were growing up to be a lot bigger these days, it was definitely no rodent.

A stack of boxes toppled over as I stumbled blindly through the dark, my hands flailing wildly in front of me. Unsure of which direction I should be heading, I blundered towards where I guessed the hatch should be. My foot caught on some scattered junk and I felt the floor rise up to meet me.

Moving on their own and fuelled by panic, my legs kicked wildly against the debris from the boxes, struggling to find a foothold. My hands thrust forwards, fingers scrabbling on the floorboards as I desperately tried to pull myself towards the dim glow of the hatch.

A splinter stabbed into my palm and I cried out in shock. My eyes were growing more accustomed to the dark now, and I saw something on the floor by my hand which chilled me to the bone. A series of claw marks had scored deep grooves in the wood.

An elastic band of fear tightened around my stomach. I

wasn't sure what could make marks like that in solid timber, but one thing was for sure, no mousetrap on Earth would hold it.

Hot tears streaked my face as I scrambled to the hatch. Kicking, crawling, dragging myself on, I finally made it to the ladder. Without hesitating, I hauled myself over the edge, tumbled head first through the hole, and landed hard on the floor.

Ignoring the sharp pain in my shoulder I leapt back to my feet and shoved the ladder up into the loft. With the steps down there was no way of closing the hatch, and with the hatch open there was nothing to stop whatever was up there following me out.

The ceiling shook when I slammed the hatch closed. My fingers refused to behave as I struggled to fasten the latch, and it took me a full thirty seconds to secure it. I stood there for what felt like forever, my hands pressed against the gloss-painted wood, listening for... something. *Anything.*

Slowly, my heart rate took its foot off the accelerator and began to return to normal. My breathing – though still heavy

– was becoming less and less panicked, too. I plucked up the courage to take my hands off the hatch. Nothing happened. No wild animals came crashing through. No monsters smashed the wood and yanked me back up. Nothing.

To be on the safe side I went into my bedroom and rummaged under the bed until I found what I was looking for. The baseball bat wasn't full-sized, but it would still be big and heavy enough to do serious damage if swung right. Even as I clutched it to me, though, I was beginning to feel like an idiot.

I flopped down on to my bed and ran back over the last few minutes. What had I actually seen? A vague movement out of the corner of my eye, that was all. A shadow, maybe; probably even my own, projected by the beam of the torch. I had been standing right in front of the light, after all.

The more I thought about it the more stupid I felt. Those scratches could have been there for decades. A heavy wooden box or piece of furniture being dragged across the floor could have made them. I closed my eyes and sighed. What a fool.

I forced out a chuckle, trying to laugh the last traces of my fear away. It had seemed easy when Mum was there, but lying on my bed on my own it was a lot harder to do. Instead I kept my eyes closed, rested my hands behind my head, and focused my attention on the breathing of the wind outside.

I don't know how long I slept for, but I know what woke me. I froze, too scared to sit up, as the ripping and rending of wood scratched at me through the ceiling.

The sound was far more frenzied and frantic than before, and each scrape seemed to bring whatever was up there that bit closer to breaking through. I tried not to picture the hands which could tear solid wood with such ease. I tried, but failed, and a detailed image of my own gory death leapt uninvited into my head.

I swung my legs down off the bed. As my feet hit the floor the sound stopped. I sat there, unmoving, wishing I'd gone with Mum. Wishing I was anywhere but in that room.

Seconds flowed into minutes as I perched there on the bed, barely daring to breathe until I was sure the scratching was over. Part of me wanted to run, but another part decided that would only draw the attention of the thing in the attic, which would be a very bad idea.

In the end I settled for a compromise, and slowly inched my way up off the bed, being careful not to let the mattress creak. When I was back on my feet I stood and listened. There was not a sound in the house. Carefully, I crept my way over to the bedroom door, the baseball bat held firmly in both hands.

Suddenly a noise from behind sent me spiralling into whole new depths of terror. I let out a shrill scream and lunged for the door, not daring to look back.

Someone was knocking on my bedroom window.

Chapter Four

THE RETURN

The stairs flew by beneath me in groups of three. By the time I was halfway to the bottom, whoever – or whatever – was outside had stopped hammering on my window. As I leapt the last few steps an eerie silence fell over the house.

For a moment I hesitated, both hands tightly gripping the baseball bat. I stood there, balanced on the balls of my feet, listening for any unexpected sound. A strong wind wailed against the stone-clad walls and whistled anxiously through invisible gaps. The front gate *clack-clacked* as it swung on its hinges, the steady beat of a solemn death march. Probably mine.

Nan had been right. The storm was building again. *Maybe going outside would be the wrong thing to do,* I figured. The sensible thing would be to stay where I was and pray to anyone who'd listen for the ordeal to be over. I could barricade myself in and wait for help to arrive. It'd be—

A fork of lightning split the night sky, filling the room with its electric glow. As the flash faded the house was once more cast into near total darkness, with only the street lights outside to ease the gloom. The electricity had gone off again. All of a sudden sticking around didn't seem like a very tempting option.

I ran for the front door, not sure where I was going, but certain I had to get out. Outside I could make it to the safety of a neighbour's house. Inside I was a sitting duck in the dark. Not even stopping to snatch up my coat, I reached for the door handle.

Just as my fingers wrapped round the cool metal a shape stepped up to the door, as if it had been standing out there just waiting to make a move. Its shadow passed across the frosted glass, blurred and impossible to make out clearly.

My shoulder slammed hard against the wood, sending a jolt of pain along my spine and making me drop the baseball bat. Gripped by panic, I pushed my weight against the door, holding it closed. The lock, which I'd used thousands of times before, was awkward and stiff in my trembling fingers, and it took all my effort to work the catch. With a concentrated effort, I finally got it to click into position as – just a few centimetres from my face – sharp knuckles rapped slowly on the door's small window pane.

'Go away!' I cried, my voice shaking as badly as my hands. I backed away from the door, not daring to take my eyes off the outline of the figure lurking outside. 'My mum's going to be home in two minutes, so you'd better get out of here!' I lied. Mum would probably still be at the home, still trying to get Nan to go with the nurses, still trying to get away. I was on my own, with someone or some*thing* standing right outside the front door!

Which left the back door clear, I realised. Whoever was outside was at the front of the house. And unless you go in through the living room and out through the kitchen, the only way to get to the back garden from the front is by going round the whole house. It's a twenty-second sprint in good conditions, so in the dark, and with the wind and rain, it'd take at least double that.

That meant I'd have a forty-second head start to get out the back and across to the next row of houses over the road. Forty seconds to get away. I almost cried with relief. I'd get out of this yet.

The rhythmic rapping stopped as I sped through to the kitchen, catching the side of the door frame and swinging myself through for extra speed. My feet found a puddle of cooking oil and I skidded and slipped my way to the back door, arms outstretched and flailing wildly to keep me from falling on my face.

Rat-a-tat-tat.

My stomach almost ejected my entire Christmas dinner as I realised I was too late.

They were already at the back door.

But nothing could have made it round that fast. It was impossible. There had to be two of them out there, that was it. Nothing supernatural about it. Just two people messing around. That's what I told myself, but whether I believed it or not is a different matter.

The key wasn't in the lock. There wasn't time to look for it, so I scrambled unsteadily over to the table and snatched up a chair. Thank God we'd taken them back through from the living room after dinner.

Struggling to stay upright on the slippery floor surface, I wedged the back of the wooden chair tight against the door handle, jamming the door tightly closed. It probably wouldn't hold them off for long, but at least it'd buy me some time to...

To what? I had no idea what I was going to do next. I'd been working on sheer adrenaline for the past five minutes, and hadn't really expected to make it this far. There'd been no time to think ahead, and now my escape routes were blocked. There was no way out of the house. I was trapped!

The steady knocking on the back door was driving me crazy. It might have had something to do with the shape of the kitchen, or the number of wooden cabinets mounted on the walls, but the knocking seemed to echo more in here, making the sound even louder.

I couldn't stand listening to it for another second. Stopping only to shove the table up against the chair for extra support,

I left the kitchen and pulled the door closed behind me. Maybe the door blocked out the sound, or perhaps the knocking stopped right at that second. Either way I couldn't hear it any more.

Back in the living room, I risked a glance at the front door. The silhouette no longer filled the little window. From here the way looked clear, but for all I knew whoever was doing this was standing just outside, waiting to grab me as soon as I stepped out into the night. That was a chance I wasn't about to take.

In the gloom, my hands searched the sideboard for the phone. This was too big to handle on my own now. I'd call Mum. Or the police. The army, maybe. Anyone who could help me. *Please*, I thought. *Someone help me*!

The handset wasn't in its cradle. *Stupid portable phone*, I cursed, looking around for any sign of the slim silver telephone. My eyes proved almost useless in the dim light, and I was forced to carry out a fingertip search of the couch, the coffee table, and every other likely hiding place.

Before I could even properly begin searching, a sharp rap of knuckles sounded on the living-room window. Frantically I hunted for the handset, too terrified to look towards the source of the sound. I was babbling incoherently, tears staining my cheeks, barely able to think. I found myself searching the same places over and over again; moving the same cushions, lifting the same pieces of scrunched and torn wrapping paper. *Where was it?!*

Another bolt of lightning tore the sky, briefly freeze-framing everything in the room. Through the window, the electric-blue light cast a long, looming shadow on the wall across from the window.

The shadow of a man in a wide-brimmed hat.

In the flash I spotted the phone sitting on top of the TV. I'd seen it in the dark, but assumed it was the remote control. A vague memory of Nan trying to switch on the telly with it earlier popped into my head, before being pushed back down again by sheer, choking terror.

Mum always forgot to put the handset back on charge and the little battery symbol was blinking at me in a way that seemed far too cheerful, given the circumstances. *'Please*,' I begged it. 'Enough for one call!'

It was nearly ten miles to the care home. The police station would be much closer. If I was lucky there'd be someone at the local one, otherwise they'd have to send someone from town. Why did I have to live in such a backwater?

Fingers shaking, eyes blurred with tears, I stabbed three nines on the keypad and held the receiver to my ear.

Nothing happened. I pulled the phone away and peered at the little LED display. The battery was still flashing, but it was hanging in there. The number was right, but it wasn't working. *Why wasn't it working?*

Trying to ignore the sound of the knocking on the window, I pressed the cancel button and redialled the number.

'Come on,' I hissed, as I waited for something to happen. 'Come on, come on, *come on*!'

After what seemed like an eternity, I heard the ringing tone I'd been waiting for. *Yes!* In just a few seconds the line gave a faint click as someone answered.

'Help me,' I begged, not even waiting for the

emergency operator to speak. 'I need the police, there's someone here. They're trying to get into my house! Please, come quick!'

An empty hiss down the line was the only reply.

'Hello?' I said into the soft static. For a moment I could hear my own voice drift off into the chasm of silence on the other end of the phone. Another failed connection? I'd have to hang up and dial again.

Before I could end the call, a low moan reached my ear, breaking up and distorting as it travelled down the telephone line.

'H-hello?' I said again. My voice echoed back to me, and I could hear my own fear.

Further moans and groans crackled from the earpiece, low and menacing, but with some urgency in their tinny tones. As I listened, I realised the sounds weren't just random groaning at all. If I concentrated I could almost make out what sounded like words. Broken words.

Mumbled words.

I concentrated harder still on the distorted, indistinct voice.

And then, suddenly, the sounds made sense. I understood them. Every word.

Time to die.

I let the handset slip from my fingers. The plastic back flew off as it bounced on the carpet, letting the tired battery ping free. A low mumbling repeated over and over in my head – *time to die, time to die, time to die...*

I jumped as the CD player suddenly sprung into life. The electricity was off, yet somehow the orange LED display on front of the machine had blinked on. Hypnotised, I watched the track number display count slowly upwards. One. Two. Three. It made it all the way to track eight, then stopped.

For a moment there was nothing but the faint *whirr* of the disk spinning, then the music began, loud enough to shake the walls. I threw my hands over my ears to protect my eardrums as Nan's Christmas hits CD kicked in.

You'd better watch out,
You'd better not cry,
You'd better not pout,

I'm telling you why,

Santa Claus is comin' to town.

My finger flew to the power button. I pressed it once, but the music played on, drowning out all other noise. Again and again I stabbed my finger against the controls, but the machine didn't respond to any of them.

Reaching down behind the player, I gave a short, sharp yank on the power cable. It would have to shut up after that.

But it didn't.

He sees you when you're sleeping,

He knows when you're awake...

My whole body shook with shock. This couldn't be happening. This was impossible.

Frantic with fear, I brought the baseball bat down hard on the CD player. The plastic casing gave a *crack*, the disk let out a deafening screech, and then silence returned to the living room.

I waited, bat raised, eyes fixed on the stereo. The storm howled outside, but inside all was quiet. Cautiously, I lowered the bat, turned away, and got back to trying to think of a way out of this mess.

Click. Over my shoulder, I heard the display on the CD player blink into life once again. Track eight kicked back in straight away. This time, though, it seemed stuck in an endless repetitive loop.

You'd better watch out, tsssk.

You'd better watch out, tsssk.

You'd better watch out, tsssk.

I lifted my leg to stamp on the machine. Suddenly, the window to my right exploded inwards, showering the room with deadly shards of glass. The couch shielded me as I threw myself to the floor behind it, my hands held protectively over my head.

As soon as the last pieces had fallen, I leapt back to my feet. A tall dark figure drew itself up to its full height on the other side of the sofa.

Another lightning bolt cast a blue aura around the figure, revealing his long dark overcoat pulled up to his ears, and his black hat pulled down almost to meet it. My mouth flapped open and closed, acting out the motions of screaming, but too choked with terror to actually manage the noise.

The figure fixed me with a beady glare and a million memories came rushing back, as if a dam had been thrown wide open in my subconscious. They were overpowering. Overwhelming. The sheer force of them nearly knocked me off my feet. They couldn't be real. It couldn't be true. *It couldn't be happening!*

Deep down, though, I knew it was. Deep down I finally understood exactly what was going on.

Mr Mumbles was back.

Chapter Five

A NEW FRIEND

I remembered.

Every line, every detail of the figure before me was... no, not the same. Familiar, but different. The Mr Mumbles of my childhood hadn't been quite like this. He had been short and skinny with friendly, shining eyes and a gift for slapstick.

His speech had always been impossible to understand, but he'd made up for it with his wide range of comedy pratfalls and skilful miming. He had been my funny little friend. My very own Charlie Chaplin.

The thing standing before me now didn't look funny at all.

The clothes were the same – the overcoat with its high collar, the curve of the hat. Parts of his face looked vaguely like I remembered – the bushy eyebrows, the big ears – but others couldn't have been more different.

His once playful eyes were dark and sunken. He'd had jolly, rosy cheeks, but now they were pale and wrinkled, like old paper. Even in the dark I could make out the spidery, dark blue lines of veins creeping below the skin.

Every detail was so lifelike. He was so real. Solid. And standing in the middle of my living room.

I'm not sure, but I think even when I was young I kind of knew Mr Mumbles wasn't real. Not *really* real, anyway. That's not to say I couldn't see him back then, but I suppose the *way* I saw him wasn't the same. He was more like a ghost I could conjure up. A supernatural spirit dressed for stormy weather, invisible to everyone but me. My best friend.

Not any more.

Sparks of hatred flashed in the dark centres of those eyes. Above them, his bushy, caterpillar eyebrows pushed down, contorting what I could see of his forehead into a twisted frown. The scowl seemed to continue down to the tip of his hooked nose, flaring his nostrils out wide.

And his lips... *Oh, God, the lips!* Mr Mumbles had always

had problems with talking, but it had been a speech impediment, that was all. Now his whole mouth was disfigured.

The lips were grotesque: thick, bloated, and sewn tightly together with grimy lengths of thread. Each stitch crossed over its neighbour, forming a series of little Xs from one side of his mouth to the other, sealing it shut. The holes the threads passed through were black and infected, the flesh rotting away from within.

My God. What had happened to him?

I should have been off and running, but I couldn't tear my eyes away from his. When I was younger, he'd been a little taller than me, but not much. Now he towered above me, easily six and a half feet in height. Up till now, the solid weight of the baseball bat had been giving me comfort, but now it felt flimsy and light, like a child's toy.

Fighting this monster was not an option.

Where before Mr Mumbles had been thin and spindly, he was now built like a bear. His densely packed frame strained the seams of his trailing overcoat. Hands the size of dinner plates clenched and unclenched into powerful fists.

His breathing was unsteady and erratic. It whistled slightly as it came down through his nose. The wind howling in through the window made his coat swish against his knees as he held me in his gaze.

The puckered skin around his lips stretched and shifted slightly as he spoke. The low, rumbling mumble was hard to make out, but I was sure I knew what he was saying. It wasn't the first time I'd heard those words tonight.

Time to die.

I feigned a move towards the back door, then shot off in the opposite direction. The sofa's wheels squeaked as I shoved it into Mr Mumbles' path and sprinted for the front door. The lock turned easily this time and I hadn't even heard Mr Mumbles make a move by the time I'd got the door open.

Suddenly, an ice-cold grip grabbed my ankle, sending me sprawling on to the front doorstep. I yelped with pain as my forearms hit the edge of the raised stone, bruising them with twin bands of purple. The baseball bat went clattering away down the garden path. But that was the least of my worries.

With his hand still tightly wrapped around my right leg, Mr Mumbles was dragging me back into the house.

I lashed out in panic, my left leg kicking violently against the chill night air. Once or twice my foot found its target and thudded against some part of my attacker. He shrugged the blows off without a word. I'm not convinced he even noticed them.

Before I knew it he was on me, his hands tight on my throat, his face almost touching mine. I could feel his weight trapping me, pinning me against the hard frosty path, smothering me. As a kid I'd been able to see him and hear him, but I'd never been able to *smell* him until now. His stench filled my nostrils; rancid and decaying, like months-old meat left rotting in the sun. I'd have choked on it if I hadn't been choking already.

My hands clawed the ground around me, searching for the baseball bat. They came back empty. Wherever the bat was, it was out of reach. I tried punching him, but he didn't flinch. I heard a rattle at the back of his throat, and realised he was laughing. His demon gaze burned into me, eyes wide, blazing with a hatred like none I'd ever seen.

His hands tightened around my windpipe. The world shimmered before my eyes, forcing me to close them. His hands tightened further still. His hands. So tight. No breath. Hands. Laughing. Choking. Choking. *Choking*.

'Hey, big ugly dude,' yelled a female voice from somewhere nearby, 'heads up!'

I forced open my eyes and peered through the checkerboard which swam before them. There seemed to be a girl walking down the garden path towards us. But that couldn't be right. Mr Mumbles raised his head.

Then, with a *crack* and a splintering of wood my baseball bat connected hard with his face. The grip released on my throat and the crushing weight left my body, as Mr Mumbles tumbled backwards into the house. Lungs almost bursting, I kicked myself backwards into the garden, gulping down mouthfuls of sweet, sweet air.

'Move!' the voice demanded, and I felt a firm hand pull me to my feet. A girl stood there – older than me, but probably not by much. The rain had matted her dark brown hair against her lighter brown skin. In her hands she held the broken remains of my baseball bat. On her face she wore an expression which said *don't make me hurt you*!

'Where to?' I gasped, still getting my breath back. Behind me, Mr Mumbles slowly sat upright.

'Anywhere but here,' the girl hissed. Without another word she turned and bounded along the path, with me in hot pursuit.

Icy rain lashed against me, numbing my face into a fixed scowl. Sheet after sheet of water battered down, blinding me. Several times I thought I'd lost sight of the mystery girl, only to find her waiting for me a little further ahead. Each time I caught up she barked that she wouldn't wait for me again. She always did.

'Who are you?' I asked on one of the times I'd caught up with her. I didn't have a lot of friends as such, but I knew who pretty much everyone in the village was. This girl wasn't from around here. I'd definitely have noticed her if she was.

'Questions later,' she hissed. 'Running away, *now*.'

We'd sprinted – and sometimes stumbled – through gardens, across roads, along winding alleys; the wind and rain trying to drive us back with every step. The warm glow of Christmas evening seeped out from the windows of almost every house we passed.

The temptation to run to any of the homes and shelter inside was almost overwhelming, but I wasn't sure Mr Mumbles would care where I hid. I suspected nothing would stop him coming for me, and all I'd be doing was putting someone else in danger. Besides, for reasons I wasn't quite sure of, the girl made me feel safe. Well, safer than I had felt before she arrived, at any rate.

My legs had begun to feel like lead as I ran down an alley between two houses and skidded to a stop at a T-shaped junction in the path. High wooden fences stretched towards the sky on both sides of a filthy alleyway. Bags of rubbish had been torn open and strewn across the sodden ground. I looked along the narrow passage in both directions. Each way the path stretched out as far as the eye could see, but the girl was nowhere in sight.

'Hello?' I hissed into the darkness. The words were swept off on the wind as soon as they'd left my lips. I tried again, louder this time: 'Hello? Girl? Where are you?'

A hand clamped down over my mouth. An arm wrapped around my throat. I struggled in vain against the grip as it dragged me through a gap between two tall fence posts and into a heavily overgrown garden.

'Shut up or you'll get us killed,' the girl growled into my ear. She waited for me to nod I understood before releasing my head from her judo hold.

We crouched down together in the long grass at the back of the garden, and held our breath. The only sound was the roar of the rain on the cracked stone slabs of the alley.

After several minutes of squatting in silence my legs began to cramp and I had no choice but to straighten up.

'Sorry,' I puffed. 'Any longer and I was going to—'

The girl flew at me, knocking me on to my back in the high grass. She squelched into the mud beside me, pulled some tall weeds down over us and held her finger urgently to her lips. I nodded again, not sure what else to do.

Slow footsteps scuffed and splashed along the alley. With a final *clack* they came to a stop right outside the garden. I'm not sure why I covered my eyes against the darkness. Maybe I thought if I couldn't see Mr Mumbles he couldn't see me. Maybe I just didn't want to see that face again. Whatever the reason, I screwed my eyes tight shut and pushed my fists hard into them until colours danced behind my eyelids.

After what felt like forever, the splashing and scuffing continued on its way. The girl put her hand on my chest to keep me from moving until she was sure the coast was clear. When she was certain he had moved on, she stood up, pulling me with her. She crept to the gate and peered along the alleyway, barely appearing to notice me.

'Is he gone?' I gulped. I held my breath as I waited for her reply. Luckily for my lungs, it didn't take long.

'He's gone,' she nodded. I breathed out again as she turned and walked back along the path in my direction. She looked me up and down as she approached, as if only now seeing me for the first time. When she was halfway back to me, she asked the question I'd quietly been hoping she wouldn't: 'Who the hell was that?'

'Just some guy,' I lied, stepping backwards into the doorway of the abandoned house, and taking shelter below the dirty plastic roof of the porch. I wasn't sure myself what was going on tonight, so there was no way I could expect anyone else to understand.

'*Right*. Just some guy,' she echoed. She was in front of me now, fixing me with eyes so brown they were almost black. 'Just some guy with embroidered lips and a violent dislike for all things you.'

'Pretty much,' I said, quietly.

'So that's it then? Just some guy? You've never seen him before in your life?'

'Nope,' I shrugged. 'Never.'

The girl narrowed her eyes and stared deep into mine. I felt myself wilt under her gaze, but I had to keep eye contact. If I looked away even for a second she'd know for sure I was lying.

'You're lying,' she said. *Damn!* How did she guess? 'You know who it is.'

'I don't!' I argued, but I was already talking to the back of her head.

'Fine,' she snapped, throwing her hands in the air as she strode away, 'don't tell me. If it wasn't for me you'd be dead, but fine, keep your little secret. Why am I even bothering to care?'

'*Mr Mumbles*,' I blurted, desperately trying to stop her leaving. She was right: I'd have been dead by now without her help, but the night was still young and there was plenty of time left to die. I'd have a better chance of surviving with her around. Better than no chance at all, at least.

She paused at the gate, but didn't look back. I cleared my throat and spoke, just loud enough to be heard over the swirling storm.

'His name's Mr Mumbles,' I explained. 'He's my invisible friend.'

Chapter Six

TRAPPED LIKE RATS

I'd expected her to laugh. She didn't. In fact, she didn't do much of anything. She just stood there, framed in the gateway, not doing or saying a thing. I think I'd have preferred it if she'd laughed.

When I was sure she wasn't going to reply I spoke again. 'Did you hear me? I said—'

'I heard you,' she answered, flatly. I watched her turn to face me once again. From her expression I could tell laughter was definitely not likely to be happening any time soon. 'I risked my life for…' she growled, before her voice trailed off into silence. When she spoke again she sounded calmer, but there was still a dangerous edge to her words which made me uneasy. 'What's your name, kid?'

'Kyle.'

'OK, Kyle, well, I want you to listen to me,' she said, advancing slowly. 'I risked my life for you tonight. I could have walked away and left you to be strangled on your front step, but I jumped to the rescue. You remember that part, right?' she scowled. 'The part where I stopped the crazy guy killing you?'

I nodded. 'Yes.'

'Good,' she said, flashing me a false smile. 'Now in doing that – in saving your life – I've put myself in danger. You with me? Crazy guy doesn't just want to kill you any more, crazy guy wants to kill me, too.'

'He might not,' I protested, weakly.

'I broke a baseball bat across his face. *I'd* want to kill me for that, if I was him.'

'Fair point.'

'Thanks,' she said, sarcastically. 'You see, Kyle, what I'm getting at – and I want you to listen to me here – what I'm saying is: This isn't a game.' She was right in front of me again, her dark eyes half covered by her darker hair, which the rain had slicked to her face. 'There's a man out there who wants to murder us, and frankly, getting murdered isn't high on my list of things to do right now. I can't imagine you're exactly sold on the idea, either.'

I shook my head. 'No.'

'Then tell me who he is, and why he was trying to kill you,' said the girl. 'The truth, this time. No games.'

I looked down at my feet and saw myself reflected in a puddle. Droplets of rain splashed into it, warping my image like a funhouse mirror. I could hear the girl's breathing, fast and unsteady. She was barely containing her anger. I raised my head and braced myself for the storm.

'His name is Mr Mumbles,' I told her. 'When I was five he was my imaginary friend. Then he went away.'

'I knew I should have kept walking,' she scowled, and she began to do just that.

'He came back,' I called after her. 'I don't know why, but he came back, and now he's trying to kill me!'

'Yeah, well you know what?' she shouted over her shoulder. 'Right now I don't blame him. I've only known you five minutes and already I'm half thinking of killing you mysel—'

The end of her sentence caught in her throat as she stepped out into the alleyway. Clumsily she stumbled backwards into the garden, struggling to stay on her feet. All the familiar feelings of fear swept over me again as I saw the panic in her movements. I knew what she was going to say even before she opened her mouth.

'He's there,' she hissed. *'He's right out there!'*

I had to see for myself. I peered out into the alleyway. Mr Mumbles was walking slowly in our direction, scanning the gardens, hunting us down. I ducked back into the garden before he could spot me.

'What do we do?' I whispered. My voice was so low and trembling I'm not even sure the words made it out of my throat.

Whether she heard or not, the girl pushed past me and grabbed hold of a wheelie bin, which lay on its side in the jungle of grass. It made a hollow boom, like a bass drum, as she stood it upright in the corner of the garden.

'Up here,' she urged, scrambling up on top of the bin. She'd positioned it next to where the fence met the back of a garage that had been built on to the side of the house. With a grunt, she pulled herself up on to the garage's flat roof. 'Now you. Come on!'

I risked a glance at the gate and was relieved to see no one there. Still, with Mr Mumbles out in the alleyway, up and over the garage roof seemed to be the only way out of the garden. Not looking back again, I ran over and began to climb.

The plastic bin was slippery in the rain. As I clambered up, my foot slipped and I dropped back down into the garden. Again I tried, and again my feet slid off the wet vinyl.

On the third try, I managed to wedge my knee against the rough stone wall and pull myself up into a standing position. The bin wobbled unsteadily beneath me, making me shift around to catch my balance. All the while I could see the girl scanning the alley behind me.

'Can you see him?' I whispered. I needed a second to

rest. Just one second to catch my breath before making the final push for the roof.

'*Yes!* He's in the garden! Move, move!'

My legs kicked furiously against the wall, and in one movement I dragged myself up on to the roof. The rough, rusted iron scraped against my knees as I spun to look back at the monster below.

Who wasn't there.

'Gotcha,' the girl sniggered. 'He went thataway,' she said, pointing back in the direction of my house. 'You can sure move fast when you need to, though.'

'What?!' I spluttered. 'You... I mean, that's... I nearly...' I gulped down a deep breath and felt my panic die down a little. 'That was just plain nasty.'

The girl nodded and grinned so hard her nose rumpled up to the size of a button. 'I know.' She got to her feet and took a few steps across the corrugated iron of the garage roof. 'Now come on, before he really does come back.'

'Is this safe?' I asked, warily. The metal was rusted into a rainbow of browns, and seemed to sag dangerously at one side. As I stood up, the whole roof complained loudly.

'Course it is,' she said. To prove her point she bounced up and down a few times. Each time she did, the metal let out a sharp squeal. 'See? There's nothing to worry—'

With a final screech of protest, a big section of the roof collapsed beneath her. For a split second she seemed to hang there in thin air, like a character in an old cartoon, before gravity sucked her down into the darkness lurking below.

I froze, not daring to move a muscle. There was no sound but the rattling of raindrops on the roof. The deluge had spent the last few days forming puddles, which now ran like rivers along the iron grooves, and down into the hole just a few feet in front of me.

'Girl?' I said, not daring to shout in case it brought the rest of the garage down on top of her. 'Are you OK?'

If she replied, I didn't hear her, but I told myself that didn't necessarily mean bad news. Even if she was shouting, I might not be able to hear her over the din of the downpour. Like it or not, I had to get closer.

Slowly, being careful not to make any sudden movements, I lowered myself down on to my hands and knees. I figured that if I spread my weight out, there was less chance of the metal buckling. Besides, I was so scared at that point I was finding it difficult to stand, so walking would have been out of the question.

Shuffling along, I edged closer to the gaping wound in the metal. Sharp, rusted edges scratched at me with every movement I made. I gritted my teeth and did my best to ignore the stabs of pain.

As I got closer to the broken section, I lay flat on my front and inched forwards on my elbows. The roof gave a few low grumbles, but otherwise seemed to be holding. With one final pull, I made it to the jagged edge of the hole.

'Girl,' I hissed. 'Are you OK?' I stared down into the garage, but only the darkness stared back. 'Girl?'

'Ameena,' came a reply from below. 'My name's Ameena.' There was a series of dull *clangs* as she clambered free from the tangle of metal she had landed in. 'And define 'OK'.'

I almost laughed with relief. She was alive and conscious, which meant she could tell me what to do. I'd known the girl for less than half an hour, but already I was placing all my faith in her. Usually it takes me a while to get to trust anyone, but I was too far out of my depth to handle tonight's events on my own, and she'd done a pretty good job of things so far.

Until she fell down the hole, obviously.

'What should I do?'

'Let me see now,' she replied. 'What should you do? What should you do? Oh, I know. How about *get me out*?'

'Right, yeah. Course,' I nodded. I thought for a few seconds, trying to ignore the freezing rivulets of rain which were trickling down my back and forming a pool at the base of my spine. It was no use. I came up blank. 'How?'

'I don't know, throw me a rope or something!'

'I haven't got a rope.'

'*Well get one!*'

'Isn't there anything down there?' I asked. 'A ladder or something?'

'As convenient as that would be,' she snapped, '*no*. And before you ask, the door's locked, too.'

'Any—'

'No. No windows, either.'

'Oh,' I muttered, defeated. 'Where will I find a rope?'

'Ropes 'R' Us? How the hell am I supposed to... *Wait!*' she cried. 'The garden. There was a washing line, wasn't there?'

'There was!' I yelped. She was right! A long length of rope had been strung between two metal poles in the garden. It was just what we needed. 'I'll go get it.'

Not thinking, I leapt to my feet. Like a wounded animal, the roof gave a desperate, deafening screech. The world lurched sideways. Something solid rose up and slammed hard against my shoulder, then did the same to my legs. I lay there, motionless, trying to blink away the shapes which danced and swam before my eyes.

'So,' sighed Ameena from somewhere beside me, 'did you get it, then?'

Something – either me or the metal I was lying on –

groaned as I stood up. Now that my vision was clearing, I could see... nothing at all.

The inside of the garage was just as dark as it had looked from up above. Even darker, if that was possible. It smelled faintly of petrol and chemicals, but the rain pouring in through the hole overhead would soon take care of that.

'What do we do now?' I ventured. 'Have you got a plan?'

'I did have,' replied Ameena, curtly. 'But it fell through.'

Stumbling through the gloom, I reached for the nearest wall. It was closer than I thought, and I smacked into it almost at once. It gave a low rumble, like distant thunder.

'That's the door,' said Ameena, her voice short and cold. 'And before you ask, yes, it's locked. The metal's quite thin, but not thin enough to break through.'

'You sure?' I asked. Determined to make up for not getting the rope, I kicked the door as hard as I could. It rang out like a church bell on Sunday morning, but otherwise didn't budge.

'Yes, I'm sure!' Ameena hissed. 'And unless you want to draw your friend's attention to the fact that we're trapped in here like rats, *don't do that again*!'

'Sorry,' I whispered, feeling stupid. Again. It was becoming a habit.

'Just sit somewhere, will you?' she sighed. 'Just... just sit down and don't move while I try to figure this out.'

'Wait, that's it!' I said.

'What's it?'

'We just sit here! We just sit right here and wait until someone comes looking for us!' I felt the hairs on my arm prickle with excitement. This was a good plan – a plan which didn't involve any more running, or any more encounters with Mr Mumbles. The *perfect* plan! 'My mum'll be home soon, and when she sees the house and realises I'm gone she'll call the police, and then they'll come find us!'

Ameena wasn't responding as enthusiastically to this idea as I'd expected her to. 'Don't you see?' I pressed. 'We can just stick it out here until we're rescued.'

'That's not a bad idea,' she whispered. 'Apart from one teensy problem.' Overhead, what remained of the roof gave an ominous creak. I looked up. Less than a metre above me, the silhouette of a man in a hat hung over the edge of the hole.

Ameena pointed at Mr Mumbles. *'Him.'*

Chapter Seven

THE BEST FORM OF DEFENCE

This time, he didn't even give me a chance to start panicking. Without a sound, he dropped down through the hole, arms outstretched, reaching for me. I half leapt, half stumbled aside, until my back was pressed up against the rear wall. The night surrounded me like a thick, black curtain, swallowing everything up, making it impossible to see. Where was he? *Where was he?*

Off to my left, Ameena cried out in shock. Instinctively, I turned in the direction of the sound, but it was no use. My visual range didn't even reach the end of my nose, let alone the other end of the garage.

She screamed in panic, but it was soft and muffled and indistinct, as if she was shouting from inside a cloud. With a start, I realised her mouth was covered. Mr Mumbles was smothering the life right out of her!

I flew at the sound, wildly flailing my arms around like windmills and screaming for him to leave her alone. After just a few steps, my fists found their target. I heard him spin to face me, and I quickly let fly with another few punches. Most of them missed, and the ones which didn't probably hurt me more than they hurt him. I kept swinging anyway.

I was still windmilling when he hit me in the chest. The blow struck like a sledgehammer. I didn't feel any pain at first, just the sensation of no longer being on my feet. Most of the air in my lungs exited in one sharp, sudden breath. What little was left was quickly knocked out when my back thudded against the garage wall.

My knees buckled, and I dropped to the floor, gasping for breath. The smell of petrol swirled up my nostrils and caught in my throat. Tiny pinpricks of light sparkled like fireflies wherever I looked. Somewhere – I couldn't even guess where – my imaginary friend let out a low, throaty laugh.

'Kyle!' Ameena yelped. 'Are you OK?'

I gave my head a shake, trying to clear the cobwebs away. A knot of pain throbbed between my eyes. Oxygen was gradually flowing back into my lungs, but my chest had begun to ache where Mr Mumbles had hit me.

'Define "OK".'

With a rustle of clothing, Mr Mumbles lunged at me. Still on my knees, I rolled sideways, and felt the wind move as he passed just above my head. Close. *Too close.*

The darkness made it impossible to know where to run. There could have been another door, or even something to fight him with, but we'd never know. We'd never find out. If only there was some sort of—

A foot splashed into a puddle at my side, and I rolled again, hoping there were no walls waiting in the direction I dived. Near the spot I'd just been, I heard a mumble of frustration. At a guess I reckoned Ameena must be somewhere to my right, keeping quiet so as not to give her whereabouts away.

Maybe we could both rush him. He was strong, but the

two of us might be able to overpower him if we worked together. Of course, to do that we'd have to be able to see him, and for that we would need—

A squeal burst from my lips as a hand caught me by the back of the neck and forced me to the ground. There was a brief flash of pain across my jaw, before the lower half of my face went cold and numb.

Icy, dirty rainwater swirled up my nose. Frantically, I blew down both nostrils, trying to keep the puddle out of my airways, until there was no air left to blow with. Automatically, my body breathed back in, and I immediately tasted filth and grime at the back of my throat.

Coughing, spluttering, I pushed back against the hand which held me, but he was too heavy, too powerful. I thrashed wildly, more terrified of the water beneath me than of the monster above.

The puddle could only have been a few centimetres deep, but that didn't matter. The water still made my pulse race and my head spin and a bubble of fear form far back in my throat.

It couldn't end like this. Not drowning, please! *Please.* Anything but drowning!

Somewhere, miles off in the distance, I could hear Ameena calling my name. Why wasn't she helping me? Why wasn't she stopping him? Couldn't she see what he was doing?

Of course she couldn't see. She couldn't see anything. None of us could see anything. I was drowning, and she was just a few feet away, and she couldn't see. Why wasn't there a light? Why couldn't there just be one—

With an electrical crackle, a bare bulb burst into life on the closest wall. I felt the hand on my neck relax just a fraction, and heard a low mumble of surprise, before Ameena launched herself at the man on my back.

Mr Mumbles caught her by the arm and swung her behind him. With a *clank* of metal, Ameena staggered into a mound of debris from the fallen roof. Out of the corner of my eye, I saw her head hit the crumpled iron, hard. She whimpered once, then slumped down on to the flooded floor.

Finding strength I didn't know I had, I twisted, knocking

Mr Mumbles off balance. He toppled sideways, and I helped him on his way with a kick to the ribs.

We both made it to our feet at the same time. Eyes locked, we stood there in the garage, the rain matting my hair and curving the brim of his hat. The light bulb buzzed on the wall, hissing quietly whenever a raindrop touched the glass. I still hadn't quite figured out where it had come from, but I wasn't about to question it. I'd needed a light, and I'd been lucky enough to get one. Now if only I could find some kind of weapon, I might stand a chance.

Almost immediately, my toe brushed against something solid on the floor. I let my eyes flick down, losing sight of Mr Mumbles for only a fraction of a second. An axe. There was a large, double-handled axe at my feet. Another coincidence? Maybe my luck was changing.

When I met Mr Mumbles' gaze again, I saw something there I hadn't seen before. Something raw and primal. Was it fear? Probably not, but I could have sworn it was something close.

Like a sprinter off the starting blocks, he made his move.

I bent double and my hands found the axe handle. It was heavy – heavy enough to do some serious damage. The silver blade glinted in the light. I gripped the smooth wood tightly. The axe felt deadly in my hands. It felt unstoppable.

It didn't stay in my hands for long. Even before I'd straightened up, Mr Mumbles wrenched it from my grip. He stood and examined it for a few moments, weighing it in his hands, studying the polished metal head, as if it were some weird, alien artefact.

Backing away, I quickly scanned the garage for something else to use against him. There was nothing. Aside from the bits of broken roof, which would be too heavy to lift, there was nothing in the garage but me, Ameena and Mr Mumbles.

And the axe in Mr Mumbles' hands.

The blade gave a low whistle as Mr Mumbles ran at me, swinging the weapon in a wide, sweeping arc. I dropped down on to my knees, as – with a *whum* – the axe cut through the air just a few millimetres above my head. A crop of neatly sliced stray hair drifted down from the top of my head.

My left knee had landed on a small scrap of the metal roof. It was barely a foot square and it was rusted badly, but it was the only thing which might be able to protect me.

I grabbed for the piece of iron and looked up in time to see Mr Mumbles bring the axe back around. The blade passed behind him, then curved up and over his hat. I blinked, unable to move, transfixed by the graceful movement of the axe, as it swung down, down, *down* towards my face.

A split second before I was split in half, the floodgates opened and reality came rushing in. I was about to die – this was no time to admire his axe-work. Recoiling, I shut my eyes tight and held up the broken section of roof for protection. It felt like a pointless gesture, but there was nothing else I could do.

The axe hit my forearm with a dull *clang*. Cautiously, I opened one eye. I couldn't quite believe what I saw.

I was no longer holding a rusted piece of scrap iron. Instead, my hands clutched a round, polished metal shield. It glinted in the glow of the bare bulb, and I could have sworn when the light reflected off the thing it actually went *ting*.

I stared at it, barely even noticing Mr Mumbles, who was also gazing at the sculpted sheet of metal that had saved me from his attack. Neither of us, it seemed, knew quite how to react.

He made his mind up before I did. With a screech, he drew back the axe and brought it down hard on the shield. The impact made my whole skeleton vibrate. I slipped my arm into the leather straps on the inside of the shield, just as he slammed down hard with another violent strike. A sharp pain shot along the length of my arm. Even with the shield protecting me, the axe was doing damage. If this didn't stop soon, it could break my arm in two.

'L-leave him alone.'

Both my imaginary friend and I turned at the same time to see Ameena getting shakily to her feet. A thick splodge of treacle-like blood clung to her hair just above her left ear, and her eyes were almost rolling backwards into her head. Despite all that, she was still trying to save me. *Me*. No one had ever even stuck up for me in school before, so this total stranger was going well beyond the call of duty.

For a second I felt a strange kind of happiness, but the now familiar feeling of utter, absolute terror soon came rushing back. Mr Mumbles had turned his back on me, and was advancing on Ameena. She staggered and slipped back down to the floor, her legs not yet strong enough to support her. I saw him raise the axe. I saw her close her eyes.

Something began to tingle at the base of my neck.

'GET... AWAY... FROM... HER!' I roared, my legs launching me forwards like springs. Mr Mumbles turned, the axe still raised above his head. I swung at him with the shield before he could bring the blade down. As the metal connected with his jaw, something like an electric shock coursed across the surface of my skull. For a split second, a bright flash filled my vision. When it cleared, Mr Mumbles was hurtling backwards, a barely recognisable blur of speed.

The metal door bent with a boom and a creak, as the monster crashed through it, tearing it free of the wall. The warped aluminium skidded and skittered along the wet driveway, before coming to rest on the road, ten or fifteen metres away. Somewhere inside the wreckage, my imaginary friend lay deathly still.

'Wow, whoever that dude is, he *really* doesn't like you,' said Ameena. I felt her hand slip into mine and braced my arm against her weight as she hauled herself up. She looked out of the garage, seeing the buckled remains of the door for the first time. 'Whoa,' she gasped. 'How did you do that?'

I stared into the empty street. Flashing lights of red and green spilled their Christmassy glow across the tarmac. Behind us, the bare light bulb went out with a fizzle and a pop. 'I don't know,' I managed, eventually. 'It just sort of... happened.'

'But it was... I mean, you... it's not...' Ameena's eyes seemed to be focusing properly now, and were open wide with shock. I knew she had a question in there somewhere that was trying to get out, but I didn't have any way to explain what I'd just done.

'It must've been a lucky punch or something,' I said.

'Come on, now that he's down we can go get the police. They can take care of him.' I chewed my lip. Could the police take care of him? Even if there was an officer on duty, would he be equipped to deal with homicidal imaginary men? I doubted it was something the local constabulary had ever had to worry about before.

'The police, are you crazy?' Ameena scoffed. All drowsiness seemed to have left her now, and – aside from the splodge of blood in her hair – she was back to her swaggering self. 'You just knocked the guy clean through a metal door. With one punch!'

I shrugged, trying my best to play it cool, despite the fact I was trembling from head to toe. 'So?'

'So when he wakes up he's going to be angry. He's going to be bloody *furious*.'

I glanced again at the twisted metal of the door. Did something move in there? Surely not. Not already.

'He'll come for you, kiddo,' Ameena warned. 'And when he does I don't think any police force on Earth is going to be able to stop him.'

Chapter Eight

MOVING THE DONKEY

There are two churches in our village. One of them is small and white and looks just like a normal house, except with a rainbow painted right across one side. The other is a big, old-fashioned spooky place, with a graveyard at the back, and a spire that looks like it might topple over at any minute. One of them is called Saint Mary's and the other is The Church of the Friendship Fellowship. No prizes for guessing which is which.

Unfortunately, the creepy one with the graveyard was closest to the garage, and Ameena decided it would be a good idea to go hide there in case Mr Mumbles came after us again.

'Why a church?' I asked.

'Because it's close,' she replied. 'And because there's not a whole lot else open right now.'

I didn't argue. I vaguely remembered reading somewhere that people used to hide out in churches for safety and protection. Right now the idea of being protected sounded pretty good.

The heavy wooden doors creaked loudly as we pushed them open. I should have expected it. Just once tonight, I'd have liked something to not sound all ominous and evil. What was it with people? Didn't anyone oil their hinges any more?

The big doors led into a low-roofed room, and a second, smaller doorway. Blue paint flaked from the walls, peeling off in large, jaggy strips, exposing the bare plaster beneath. The place smelled exactly like the attic at home, and for a moment the stench of damp triggered the first stirrings of panic, before I was able to swallow it back down.

I'd never been in a church before – Mum didn't believe in 'any of that nonsense' – but from everything I'd heard about them, I was expecting something a bit more grand and impressive. This was just like a corridor – a narrow space with a tatty rug on the floor and a cork-board on one side with some boring-looking notices pinned to it.

'It's like a shed or something,' I muttered.

Then Ameena stepped past me and pulled open the second set of doors.

At once, I realised my mistake. A long aisle of polished wood shone all the way from the entrance to an imposing statue of a giant Jesus on the cross. Around the hall, the walls curved up and up, until they became the thick, oak beams of a vast, ornate ceiling.

From the ceiling hung two huge chandeliers, which looked like they'd been made to hold candles, but which were now rigged up with dozens of little light bulbs. Their soft white glow cast a strange, almost magical sheen over the rows and rows of wooden pews.

In all directions, stained-glass saints looked lovingly down from the windows, watching over the congregation from worlds away. Right now, though, the congregation consisted of Ameena, me and not another living soul.

'You must have a really impressive shed,' she whistled, stepping into the church. Her footsteps echoed on the wooden floor, and the sound seemed to bounce all the way around the room.

'Pretty amazing, eh?' I said, my voice hushed.

'Not too shabby,' she admitted, quietly. 'But why are you whispering?'

'I don't know,' I shrugged, still keeping the noise down. 'Aren't you supposed to whisper in churches? Isn't that like a rule or something?'

'I think that's libraries.'

'Oh, yeah.'

We were still speaking in hushed tones, neither one of us daring to be the first to raise our voices.

'I really want to shout,' Ameena said. She giggled, nervously. It was the first girly thing I'd seen her do. 'Like, properly shout, just to see what happens.'

'Don't!' I hissed. 'You'll get us chucked out!'

'By who? There's no one here but us and the Big J over there.' She glanced across at the enormous statue. 'And I can't see him grassing us up.'

'Look, just don't, will you?' I pleaded. I wasn't used to churches, and they made me uneasy. With everything I'd been through already tonight, I didn't know if my nerves could take any more strain.

'Fine, I won't,' Ameena sighed, 'but only if we stop whispering.'

'OK,' I agreed, still hushed. 'Just don't shout!'

'Right, then,' she said, in something closer to her normal volume. 'There, I've done it. Your turn.'

'What should I say?' I asked, quietly.

'It doesn't matter! Just say anything.'

'Anything,' I said. My voice sounded stupidly loud in the silence of the church hall.

'There, wasn't so bad, was it?'

I shrugged. It still felt wrong to be speaking out loud in a church, but then I figured that people sang hymns and stuff there, so talking was probably allowed, too. I also had a vague memory of a man who came to visit our school two or three times a year. He wore a black suit and a white dog collar, and spoke as if everyone else in the world was deaf. If he was allowed in a church, then speaking in a normal voice couldn't possibly be against the rules.

Ameena nodded and smiled as she scraped her hair away from her face and tied it back. It was the first time I'd been able to look at her properly since she'd shown up. To begin with I'd thought she was older than me, but now I wasn't so sure. A little taller, yes, but maybe my age.

Her skin was pale brown, like coffee with milk in. She was skinny – a little bit too skinny to be healthy – and I wondered where she'd found the strength to hit Mr Mumbles so hard with my bat earlier in the night. Adrenaline, I guessed.

Her clothes were shades of black and grey, and looked like they'd been slept in. But so did mine right now, so I couldn't exactly blame her for that. Either her feet were ridiculously out of proportion to the rest of her body, or the shabby black boots she wore were a good few sizes too big. Either way, I imagined getting a kick from one of them would be like being booted by a horse.

I watched her set off to explore the church. Living in the

middle of nowhere, I didn't get to meet a lot of people. It was usually the same faces saying the same things, day after day after day.

Ameena was different. Not just because she was new, but because she was... well, just *different*. I'd never met anyone like her before. I doubted there was anyone else quite like her *to* meet.

It was lucky she'd shown up when she had. Another one of tonight's coincidences that I didn't want to start questioning too much. That said, though, there was something about her... Something about the way she was taking most of the weirdness in her stride, which made me wonder if—

'Hey, check these out,' she called, waving at me from the closest corner of the hall and derailing my train of thought. I jogged across and found her standing stock-still, pretending to be part of the full-sized nativity scene which had been set out in the corner nearest the door. She stood there, hands clasped together, between the Three Wise Men and the shepherds, and just behind a donkey with an ear broken off.

'You make a good angel,' I told her. Instantly, a blush

stung at my cheeks. That sounded like a corny chat-up line. 'I mean... I didn't...'

'I'd make a terrible angel,' she replied, choosing not to comment on my remark. 'Feathers freak me out.' Her whole body convulsed at the thought of them. Nope, I'd definitely never met anyone like Ameena before.

When her shuddering had passed, she rapped her knuckles on the donkey's ribcage. 'What do you think of this baby?' she asked.

'It's... a donkey?'

'It's not just a donkey, kiddo, it's a *heavy* donkey.'

I looked from the statue of the animal to Ameena and back again. She was nodding like she was trying to tell me something, but I didn't have a clue what it was.

'So?'

'*So*, super strength, remember?'

'Nope, you've lost me.'

Ameena threw up her arms and let out a dramatic sigh. 'Look, you punched a full-sized man through a metal door, right?'

'Like I said, it was a lucky punch, that was—'

'Shut up, I'm not finished. Lucky punch or not, what you did shouldn't have been possible. Under any normal circumstances, a weakling like you – no offence – should not have been able to do something like that.' She paused for a moment, letting her words sink in. Much as I'd have liked to, I couldn't argue.

'Meaning that for a split second there, you used muscles you don't even have. For just that moment, you were strong. *Super* strong.' She gave the donkey statue a shove. It didn't budge. 'Aren't you even a little curious how you did it?'

'Not really, no.'

'Liar! Come on, have a go. See if you can lift it. It could come in handy for when your friend gets back on his feet.'

She had a point. Something *had* happened to me when I'd run at Mr Mumbles. Something I didn't remember ever feeling before. I thought about the tingling at the top of my spine, the feeling of electricity crackling across my skull. Something had definitely been happening to me. The question was: What?

And then there was the other stuff. The light bulb which burst into life just when I'd needed it most. The axe which had appeared out of nowhere. And as for the shield...

I decided to keep those bits to myself. Ameena could have bumped into the light switch. The axe could have been there the whole time, for all I knew, and the shield... OK, the shield was a little harder to find an explanation for, but given time I'd think of one. It was all just a series of silly coincidences. There was nothing strange about it.

Except that I'd hit Mr Mumbles like an express train. There was no way of getting around that one.

'OK,' I nodded, at last. 'Let's do it.'

Veins I didn't know existed bulged on my forearms, standing out like thick blue wires from the skin around them. The whole area from my wrists to my elbows felt as if it was being burned up from the inside. Any minute now I half expected to see smoke pouring from my fingertips.

Gritting my teeth, I dug my toes into the wooden floor and heaved harder, until my entire body was trembling from the strain. I'd been telling myself for the past five minutes that I could do this, but it was starting to look as if I was wrong. Try as I might, I just couldn't budge the donkey.

'Come on, put your back into it,' Ameena barked. Easy for her to say. She was perched up on top of the nativity stable, one leg dangling over either side of the pointed roof.

'*I am* putting my back into it,' I puffed. 'It's no use. It's too heavy.'

'How hard can it really be to lift one little stone donkey?'

'You come down here and try it, then, if you think it's so easy!'

'Ah,' she grinned, 'but I'm not the one with the magic mega-muscles, am I?'

'Neither am I,' I sighed. 'It was just—'

'A lucky punch, yeah, so you keep saying,' she snorted. She shuffled towards the front edge of the roof, then jumped down to join me.

'Careful,' I warned, 'you nearly landed on the baby Jesus.'

'So? It's just a doll.'

'I know, but... it's probably unlucky or something.'

Ameena looked at me, her mouth curving into a smirk. 'It's unlucky to jump off a shed and land on a doll?'

'Yeah,' I nodded, convincing no one. 'If... the doll's Jesus.'

'I see,' she replied. 'I'll be sure to keep that in mind.'

She gave the donkey statue a slap on the backside and winked at me. 'Now, let's give this another go.'

'It's a waste of time,' I protested. 'I can't lift it.'

'Then try harder. You must be doing something wrong.'

'Listening to you, that's what I'm doing wrong!' I cried. I was annoyed enough that I couldn't move the thing. I didn't need her rubbing it in. 'I should be at the police station, telling them everything, not here giving it Mr Universe!'

'*What?* If you hadn't listened to me you'd be dead by now!'

'Yeah? Well...' I floundered, struggling to find a decent comeback. 'So?'

'So?' Ameena scoffed. 'That's the best you can come up with? *So?* You know what your problem is, Kyle? You've got no imagination.'

'No imagination?' I yelled. 'In case you've forgotten, something I *imagined* was just trying to murder us both! Imagination-wise, I'd say that's pretty bloody impressive, wouldn't you?'

'Then move the donkey!'

'But my imagination's got nothing to do with—'

'*Move the donkey!*'

'*Fine! I'll move the damn—*'

BOOM!

In a spectacular shower of dust and plaster, the statue of the donkey exploded before our eyes. I stood, rigid and staring, feeling tiny invisible threads of electricity dart backwards across my head and down my neck.

For a long time there was no sound in the church, other than the echo of the explosion. Even the wind and rain appeared to pause in their onslaught. At last, the floor gave a faint creak, as Ameena nervously shifted her weight from one foot to the other. She brushed some stone dust from her hair.

'Well,' she began, 'I think we can safely consider the donkey moved.'

I didn't reply. Instead, I closed my eyes and concentrated on the tingling sensation which still zapped through my scalp. It was a strange feeling. I'd thought it was completely new, but now I realised it wasn't completely unfamiliar.

I'd felt it a few times that night, but it had been there maybe a dozen times in the months before then, lurking quietly at the back of my brain. If I could somehow hold on to it this time – somehow stop it slipping away – then maybe I could figure out what it was.

The dim light behind my eyelids swirled in slow circles, reminding me of the satellite images of tornadoes I'd seen on the news. Every so often, a spark of white or blue would flash like a fish in a stream, before vanishing back down into the dark waters of my mind.

'Kyle?' I heard Ameena say, but I ignored her. When she spoke again she sounded distant and garbled, as if talking on a radio that was tuned to two different stations at once. Whatever she was saying, it could wait.

I focused on the flashes, trying to slow them down enough for me to see them properly. All the while, the electrical tingling crept through my hair. It had changed direction and was creeping forwards again – a silent predator, edging closer and closer to the front of my head.

Flash. A white spark shot past.

Flash. A blue one passed by, slower, buzzing like a wasp.

Flash. Blue again. This time I was too fast for it. As it sparked behind my eyes I concentrated like I'd never concentrated before, focusing all my attention on that one, tiny bright spot.

The little blue lightning bolt buzzed angrily, trapped like an insect in a jar. It vibrated in the darkness, but it could struggle all it liked. It wasn't going anywhere. I'd done it. I'd managed to hold on to one of the sparks!

I was just about to congratulate myself, when the screaming started. It sounded frantic – deranged, even – but it didn't sound like Ameena. It didn't even sound human.

My concentration broken, the blue flash zipped gratefully off into the darkness once more. I flicked opened my eyes, and gasped. There before me lay a vision of hell.

Chapter Nine

THE DARKEST CORNERS

Almost at once, the screaming stopped. I barely noticed it come to an end.

Around me, the church stood in ruins. The imposing brick walls lay crumbled and wrecked; the stained-glass windows shattered from their frames. Just moments ago I had been standing on polished wood, but now a carpet of weeds and grass tangled around my feet.

The chandeliers were gone. No surprise, as they no longer had a roof to hang from. Up above me, a billion unfamiliar stars looked down from a cloudless sky, occasionally winking, as if they all knew something I didn't.

Ameena. Where was Ameena? She'd been there beside me, but now... I whispered her name into the darkness, but no reply came back. She wasn't here. I was on my own.

Or was I?

Through one of the gaps in the collapsed wall, I could see a street. Dark, misshapen figures skulked, stalked and skittered back and forth across the road, illuminated here and there by the flickering flames of burning wreckage.

Keeping low, I crept across to a mound of rubble, crouched down behind it, and peeked through a gap. None of the people – no, they weren't people, they couldn't be people – none of the *things* which were moving around outside seemed to know I was there, so if I could stay out of sight for long enough I might be able to figure out what the hell was going on.

The street outside was the same one Ameena and I had run along to get to the church, only now – like the church itself – it was completely different. The houses which lined either side of the road had all been either boarded up or torn down. Those which were still standing appeared to throb and move as if alive.

It was only when I looked more closely that I realised the

effect was caused by hundreds of insect-like creatures, which crawled as one over every surface, poking and prodding at the barricaded windows as they tried to find a way in.

The things out on the street, on the other hand, didn't seem to be moving with any shared purpose. Some seemed to be in an incredible hurry. They would appear from an alleyway on one side of the street, and then in the blink of an eye would disappear into another across the road.

Other figures were in less of a rush. These ones took their time. They strolled lazily along the length of the street, stopping occasionally at the flaming remains of a car, warming themselves, or maybe just appreciating the destruction.

Still others were involved in brief, violent battles which came out of nowhere. Groups of two or three of the creatures would suddenly lunge and begin tearing each other to pieces. I watched, dumbstruck, as one spindly figure was torn clean in half by two larger beasts. It thrashed and howled like a demon, and I realised this was the screaming I had heard just before I'd opened my eyes.

What were they? I couldn't be sure. A lot of them were vaguely human-shaped, but even from this distance it was clear that none of them were *all the way* human. They were either too large or too small, had too many arms, too many heads or too many *tails* to qualify as a member of the human race.

Some of them wore clothes – dirty, torn rags for the most part, serving very little purpose. The naked ones moved like animals, scurrying around on however many limbs they happened to have.

Categorising them like that was wrong, though. They couldn't be divided into humanoid and non-humanoid, or naked and clothed, or anything like that. They couldn't be categorised at all, because not one of them looked the same as the others.

I saw one creature covered in thick, coarse hair, another with scaly skin that shimmered in the pale moonlight. Yet another slithered along the street, leaving a silvery, slug-like trail in its wake.

They roared. They whispered. They hissed and howled.

Some laughed. Others sobbed, or snarled, or screeched or screamed.

Watching them, I realised there was one category they could all fit into. One word that could be used to describe them all:

Hideous.

Tears ran down my cheeks as I turned away and slunk down behind the rocks. What had happened? The church, the street – probably even the whole village – had been turned into some twisted, hellish version of itself, but how? And where was Ameena? Was she here somewhere, too?

All those questions. So many questions which I couldn't answer. But there was another question, too – one I hardly dare ask myself: had I done this? Was it all somehow my fault?

It couldn't be, I told myself. *How could I have possibly done this?* No matter how much I tried to convince myself, though, the thought remained, lurking quietly at the back of my mind.

I decided that what I needed was a plan. Well, what I

really needed was a miracle, but a plan would be the next best thing. If I had a plan then I'd have something to focus on, other than the hundreds of creatures which lurked outside.

First thing first – I had to find out if the rest of the village was like this too. Maybe whatever had happened was contained to just this one street. Maybe there were other people – real, normal people – just round the next corner. If I could find them, we could figure everything out together.

So I had a plan, although admittedly it wasn't without its problems. For starters, I could see thick plumes of greyish smoke billowing up from at least the next few streets over. That didn't bode well for the theory that it was only this one which had been affected by... whatever was going on.

The second, perhaps even bigger flaw in the plan, was that to get to the next street I'd have to get past this one. And doing that may well put me into direct contact with the monstrous things roaming about.

Still, my mind was made up. Flawed or not, it was the only plan I could think of, and anything was better than sitting here, waiting to be found. Well, no, I could think of lots of things worse, but waiting to be found was still pretty grim.

Moving as quickly as I dared, I crept on my hands and knees towards the back wall of the church, picking my path carefully through the overgrown undergrowth. Overhead, something swooped down low on large leathery wings. Not daring to look up, I listened to it circling round a few times, before, with a low gargling sound, it continued on its way.

The back of the church led out into the graveyard. Normally, going into a cemetery in the middle of the night would be near the bottom of my list of Things To Do, but, spooky as the graveyard might be, it wouldn't come close to what was going on at the front.

When I reached the mound of bricks that used to be the back wall, I stopped and peeked outside. The graveyard was there, and, as I'd hoped, it was completely deserted.

After pausing for a second to steady my nerves, I clambered over the rubble, slid down the other side, and began to run towards the wrought-iron fence which surrounded the burial ground.

The grass crunched underfoot as I ran, my shoes leaving imprints in the frost. I realised for the first time that it wasn't raining, and by the looks of things it hadn't been for some time. Last I'd checked, it had been pouring for weeks. What was going on?

There was no time to think about that now. Weaving and dodging past a dozen moss-covered headstones, I made it to the fence, and squeezed myself sideways through a gap where a bar should have been.

I emerged into a thick knot of trees. Their spindly branches scratched at my face as I pushed my way through the foliage. This wasn't right. The back of the graveyard should have brought me out on to Wilkinson Road. From there I was only along two streets and up the hill to my house. So where had the trees come from? Why was there a forest where a road should have been?

I pushed through the undergrowth and took a few hesitant steps forwards, trying to get my bearings. Before I could figure it all out, something lurking in the brush a short distance to my left gave a low, threatening growl. I hesitated,

122

all my questions already forgotten, as my survival instincts debated over whether to stand still or make a run for it.

With a faint rustle of leaves and a snapping of twigs, whatever was hidden in there began to creep closer – slowly, at first, then gradually faster, until I could see the grass being pushed aside in its wake. A low, squat shape appeared briefly above the scrub, before ducking down again as it crashed towards me.

Decision made. I turned on my heels and ran. Close behind, the unseen creature spat out an angry snarl and plunged after me, closing the gap with every step.

The trees snagged and snared me as I fled, clawing at me, trying to slow me down. I threw up my arms to protect my face, but soon the palms of my hands were raw and bleeding from the forest's assault.

A sound – somewhere between a bark and a squeal – snapped at my heels and I hurried on, forcing my aching legs to give me more speed. My muscles burned from the effort.

But it wasn't enough.

With a roar, the pursuing animal leapt on to my back, knocking me forwards. Sharp claws scraped across my flesh. I managed to cry out in pain and shock before I hit the ground in a clumsy forward roll.

Our combined momentum carried both me and the creature on, flipping us over and trapping it beneath me. It shrieked and lashed out wildly, and I caught sight of a deformed, clawed hoof as it swiped at my face. Hot, angry breath hit the back of my neck, and I imagined unseen jaws getting ready to snap shut.

Quickly, I fired a sharp elbow at the beast. It howled, and thrashed harder still. Again and again I drove my elbows down into its twisting body, until with a damp *crack* something inside it gave way.

At once, the animal became less interested in attacking, and more worried about getting out from under me. It kicked furiously with its back legs, pushing against the ground, trying to squeeze out from where I had it pinned. I wasn't about to argue.

Leaping to my feet, I sprinted off through the forest, not

chancing a look back at the shrieking, wounded beast I had left behind.

Further and further I blundered into the woods, all sense of direction now long gone. Still I ran, stumbling through the dark, too afraid to stop in case another of the creatures found me.

Something in the undergrowth hit me at around knee height, and I leapt backwards; fists raised; ready for anything.

Almost anything.

A moss-covered rectangle jutted up from the grass. It stood there, barely three feet high; still and silent, showing no sign of moving.

Cautiously, I pulled aside some of the grass that was concealing the object. The moss came off in dirty clumps when I scraped at it, revealing a sheet of metal underneath.

The metal looked as if it had once been white, but now was stained in streaks of greens and browns. I tore off another handful of the moss and revealed a large, black letter W.

More of the moss came away in my hand, uncovering

other letters. Some were faded and peeling, but before long I was able to make out the entire sign. I stared down at it, shocked but not exactly surprised.

Wilkinson Road. I knew it. I just wasn't sure why it was now buried under an acre of forest.

I pushed on towards where I hoped my own street would be, although the high trees on all sides meant I was working almost entirely on guesswork. Somewhere to my left, the screaming had started again, so I curved to the right, keeping as much distance from the sound as I could.

And then suddenly I was falling; rolling, tumbling out of the trees, down a steep embankment which had come at me out of nowhere. Desperately, I reached out, grabbing for something – *anything* – that would slow my descent, but any handhold I found slipped swiftly through my fingers.

A split second before I hit it, I caught a glimpse of a dark pool of water. I barely had time to draw in a deep breath, before I plunged below the still, stagnant surface. My heart thudded and my mind raced. *Not water. Please, not water!*

I hate water. I hate it so much that just being close to it

makes me want to throw up. Here, now, surrounded by it – *sinking* in it – a panic gripped me.

My heart raced. My lungs burned holes in my chest. I kicked my legs, flailed my arms. Desperately. Frantically.

But it was no use. The faint light rippling on the surface above me faded as I sunk down into the waiting depths.

I was floundering so much I barely noticed my feet touch the bottom. The ground was muddy and soft, but I was able to dig my toes into it until they found something solid.

The water tried to force me back as I kicked upwards. I couldn't swim, but the kick-off had given me a good start. I clawed with my hands and thrashed with my legs until my head exploded up above the surface.

The night air tasted smoky and bitter as I swallowed it down, but I didn't mind. I kicked my legs and managed to clumsily keep myself afloat long enough to take in my surroundings.

The water was filling what looked like a man-made hole in the ground. The pit was rectangular, about the length and width of a bus. It could have been a small swimming pool, but who'd build a swimming pool here?

I struggled over to the edge and hauled myself up on to the hard, uneven ground. I crawled on for several metres, trying to get as far from the water as I could. Finally, my exhausted arms gave out and I rolled on to my back.

For a few long moments I lay there, breathing heavily, gazing up at the unfamiliar night sky. My soaking body shook with the cold. The sharp ache from the scratches on my shoulders mixed with the dull throbs of my fall, to form an all-encompassing wave of pain. I knew, though, that I didn't have time to sit around feeling sorry for myself. As quickly as I could manage, I drew myself up into a sitting position.

A girl of around five years old stood before me, peering out from behind a curtain of long black hair. Her skin was pale, but caked with grime and muck. Her eyes appeared to be almost too large for her face – two impossibly dark pools, boring a hole straight through me. Around each one was a dark smudge of eye shadow. Across her lips was an uneven streak of red lipstick. Childish attempts at looking like an adult.

In her hands she clutched a bundle of rags. No, not just

rags – a doll made of rags. Scrawny arms and legs dangled down limply from its stuffed torso. Its head hung low, but as the girl stepped closer, I could have sworn the thing turned to look at me. A brief flash of a cracked porcelain face was all I saw, but it was enough to give me the willies.

'Have you seen Billy?' the girl asked. Her voice was high and soft, but completely unafraid, which caught me off guard.

'Billy?' I replied, unsure of what else to say. The only Billy I knew was Billy Gibb, a boy in my year in school who I didn't really get on with. She couldn't mean him, surely? 'I don't... I don't think so.'

'Billy used to play with us,' she continued, her gaze still fixed on me, 'but then he sent us away. He doesn't like us any more.'

'I'm sure that's not true,' I said, edging backwards on my hands. She was just a little girl – probably lost in this hell-hole, like me – but every time she spoke it felt as if my skin was trying to crawl off my bones.

'Billy made me sad,' sang the girl, swinging the doll back

and forth by its arms. Every time it swung towards me, the head lifted enough for its eyes to meet mine. 'When I get sad, Raggy Maggie gets *very* cross.'

The girl's arms stopped, and the doll's pendulum movement slowed almost at once. Frowning, she lifted its mouth to her ear and listened, her stare never once shifting from me.

'But he says he doesn't know where Billy is.' I watched, hypnotised, as she moved the doll's head up and down at her ear. 'Oh, no, I'm sure he wouldn't tell nasty lies to us, would you?'

'N-no,' I stammered. I wanted to move, but something about the girl's stare had turned my arms and legs to lead.

'Raggy Maggie has something she wants to tell you,' the girl whispered. 'She says it's something very important.' She reached out her arm, holding the doll so its face was just centimetres from mine.

Up close, it was even creepier than I'd first thought. Like the girl, the doll's face was pale white, but stained here and there by black and grey smudges of filth.

Thin wisps of straw blonde were all that remained of its hair – dirty and matted and messy. A dark crack ran from the top of her ceramic head down through her left eye. Her one good eye seemed to follow me as I pulled away.

A voice which wasn't her own suddenly came out of the girl's mouth – screechy and harsh, like fingernails being dragged down a blackboard. As the girl nodded the doll's head up and down, the doll's voice spoke three simple words:

'*He's behind you.*'

Chapter Ten

THE FIRST MEETING

I turned, spinning up on to my knees, half expecting Mr Mumbles to come leering at me from the shadows. Instead, a middle-aged man with dark hair and smiling brown eyes extended a hand towards me, palm upwards, as if to help me up.

I looked at him suspiciously. He was human, at least. That was something. And his smile appeared genuine.

Cautiously, I placed my hand in his. His grip was as strong as his skin was rough, and he lifted me to my feet with no effort at all.

Even standing, I fell a good few centimetres short of the man's shoulders. He towered above me, big and broad beneath his red-checked lumberjack shirt, like a rugby player.

Despite the man's size, for the first time in hours I didn't feel threatened or afraid.

'Hey, kiddo,' he smiled, looking me up and down. 'Maybe I'm wrong, but it looks to me like you're a long way from home.'

'I... don't know,' I replied, hesitantly. 'I'm not sure.'

'Trust me,' he said. 'You are.'

I nodded, not really wanting to argue.

'Good job I found you when I did,' the man continued. 'There's some nasty things out there.'

I suddenly remembered the girl. When I turned round, she was nowhere to be seen.

'There was a girl,' I told him, 'a little girl. With a doll.'

'Ah, that would be Caddie,' the man said, nodding solemnly. 'One of them nasty things I was just talking about. Best avoided.'

I glanced back at the spot where Caddie had stood, and felt an icy shiver travel the length of my spine. 'I will.'

'She's not the worst, but it's probably just easier and safer all round if you keep out of her way.'

I nodded. He didn't have to tell me twice. I'd be happy never seeing the girl again. 'Where... what is this place?' I asked, taking in my new surroundings for the first time.

The pool of water was a few feet behind the man. Beyond that was the hill I'd rolled down. The forest stood at the top of it, ominous and silent.

Around me seemed to be nothing but waste ground. Dark, oily puddles pitted the soil like blackheads. Mounds of scrap wood and metal lay abandoned all around, some scorched and burned, others presumably just waiting to be.

'The Darkest Corners,' said the man.

'The what?'

'The Darkest Corners,' he repeated. 'Charming, isn't it?'

'I've never heard of it,' I replied, shaking my head.

'Not many have,' he shrugged. He hooked his thumbs through the belt loops of his jeans and leaned back on his heels. 'In fact, apart from those living here, I'd say you're probably the first.'

'But...' My mind raced with a thousand questions, none of which wanted to wait their turn. 'I don't get it. At first I thought it was my village, but then, I mean now... I don't know.'

'Yeah, it can be confusing like that,' he agreed. 'I remember my first visit. Not nice. Brought on a panic attack that lasted about a fortn—' A strangled hiss from nearby broke his sentence in two. He held up a hand for silence, and listened to the whistling of the wind. Though the sound didn't come again, his face remained grave with concern. 'It's not safe out here for you,' he warned. 'You'd best come with me.'

He led me across the waste ground, speaking only twice to warn me of possible danger ahead. Both times nothing materialised, and soon we were sneaking along the side of a low, stone building with barricaded windows and boarded-up doors.

At the third or fourth window, the man stopped. He told me to keep my eyes open for danger, then he knocked out a complex series of beats on the wooden planks.

To begin with, I didn't think anything was happening. We stood there, close together, neither one of us saying a word. Eventually, I could hear the sound of footsteps within the building, drawing closer. After a few seconds, a dozen or more bolts were slid noisily back, and the entire window blockade swung inwards.

'Go,' the man nodded, stepping aside to let me through. I

pulled myself in through the gap, and began to slide head first towards the floor on the other side.

Just before I hit the ground, a hand caught me by the arm. It dragged me away from the window, hauling me upright as it did. I found myself looking at a hooded figure, just slightly taller than myself. The person underneath had their head and face hidden beneath a long, flowing robe, and I couldn't even tell if they were male or female.

'See to the window,' the man who had helped me said, sliding down through the barricade behind me. The robed figure nodded, and immediately set about fixing the boards back into place. 'The things out there don't usually attack here,' he said, turning to me, 'but with you inside, I can't be sure. You'd be a prize catch.'

I followed behind him as he began to march off along a wide corridor, which was lit at irregular intervals by tall, floor-standing gas lamps. Beneath my feet, the dusty carpet felt threadbare and thin, and made a sound like *fup-fup-fup* as we walked along it.

'What are those things, anyway?' I asked. I felt better when I was talking. Talking left less time to think. 'They didn't even look human.'

'That's because they *aren't* human,' he replied, matter-of-factly. 'Never have been. Most of them are nothing more than shadows. Ghosts of the past. All of them are lost. Neglected. *Forgotten.*' He spat out that last word, as if it had left a foul taste in his mouth.

'I see,' I nodded, despite the fact I didn't have the faintest idea what he was on about.

'You don't have the faintest idea what I'm on about, do you?'

I stopped for a moment, shocked, then doubled my pace in order to catch up with him again. 'How did you do that?' I demanded.

'Do what?'

'How did you know what I was thinking? You read my mind!'

'Well now,' he grinned, 'that's hardly any great achievement *here* of all places, is it?'

Before I could question any further, he pushed open a heavy wooden door and stepped inside. I followed him through, and we emerged into a startlingly familiar room.

'This...' I muttered, looking around at my own carpet, my own curtains, my own bed. 'But, this is my room.'

'An impression of it, anyway,' the man nodded, sitting on my bed. He leaned back, shook his head once, and smiled at me. 'I've got to tell you, kiddo, I can't believe you're actually here. I mean, I knew you were going to be powerful, but to make it here without any help? Without any practice?' A low whistle escaped his lips. 'That's something.'

I frowned. The man was making less and less sense every time he opened his mouth. 'Sorry?' I said. 'I don't know what you mean.'

'OK, so not the sharpest knife in the drawer,' he chuckled, 'but powerful? You bet.' He leaned forwards so he was perching right on the edge of the bed. 'I'm telling you, I've got a great feeling about this, Kyle.'

The last word hung there in the air, flashing a furious red.

'How do you know my name?'

'I know all there is to know about you, Kyle,' he said. Suddenly his smile didn't seem quite so friendly any more, and the room, familiar as it was, no longer felt safe. 'Tell me. How did you like the present I sent you?'

'What present?'

'*The* present!' he yelled, jumping to his feet. He stepped closer, excitement blazing behind his eyes, and clamped his big hands on to my arms. It didn't hurt, but it felt like it could if he wanted it. 'The best present you've ever had! The last present you'll ever get!'

'I don't know what—'

'What was it you called him again? Oh yes.' His grip on me tightened just a fraction. 'Mr Mumbles.'

At the mention of the name, my not-quite bedroom began to spin around me. I swallowed, but my mouth and throat felt desert dry. 'What did you say?'

'Wow, that guy hates you!' the man laughed. 'I mean, don't get me wrong, I'm not exactly your number one fan either, but Mumbles? Man, does he have a grudge! Course, can't say I blame him, the way you treated him.'

'Wh-who are you?' I asked.

'If only you knew,' he smirked. He let go of my arms and turned away.

'Tell me.'

'Consider me a teacher,' he replied, turning back to face me. The smile was gone from his face now, and his expression was cold and stern. 'And think of Mr Mumbles as your first lesson. If you can beat him – and I'll be honest here, Kyle, I don't see that happening – but if you can beat him, you'll pass the test, and we can move on to lesson two. Pass all the tests, and maybe – *maybe* – you'll be worthy.'

I wasn't sure I wanted to know the answer, but I had to ask. 'Worthy of what?'

His eyes glinted as he leaned his face in close to mine. 'Worthy of helping me bring about the end of your world.'

My eyes flicked everywhere around his face, unable to hold his gaze. 'What? What do you mean?'

'You know what?' he sighed, leaning back. 'Fun as this has been, I'm bored now. It's just the same questions with you, over and over, isn't it? So if you'll just...' He caught me by the shoulders again, and spun me around so my back was to him. In the doorway, the hooded figure held up a small, wooden box. It gave an almost inaudible squeal, then nearly blinded me with a powerful flash of white light.

'Great stuff,' the man said, releasing me from his grip. 'Now, get out of my house.'

'W-what?' I stammered. 'But it's—'

He ran at me, a blaze of fury, the sinews on his neck sticking out like thick, red ropes. '*GET OUT OF MY HOUSE!*'

I opened my eyes with a start and found Ameena staring down at me, her face a mask of concern. I heard her sigh with relief when she saw that I was awake.

'Don't do that to me!' she gasped. 'You're such a freak!'

'D-do what?' I muttered, trying to get to grips with my surroundings. I could feel cool, varnished wood at my back. Overhead, a chandelier swung gently back and forth on a current of invisible drafts. I was in the church. The real church. Thank God.

'Wander off like that,' she said. 'I turn my back for one second and what, you run off and hide? Took me nearly ten minutes to find you.'

I glanced around and realised I was lying between two long pews, my body half-hidden beneath one of them. I was only a few paces from where I'd been standing, but from the aisle I would have been almost impossible to spot.

'I… I didn't hide.'

'So I see,' Ameena nodded, and I thought I could detect just a hint of concern in her voice. 'What happened? You pass out or something?'

'Must have.'

'Well… at least you're OK. Now tell me,' she said, 'how did you *do* that?'

'Do what?' I frowned. I sat up and immediately wished I hadn't. The world lurched and spun, and I spent the next few seconds swallowing back at least three mouthfuls of sick.

'You blew up the donkey! It was *amazing*!'

When I could focus properly, I looked up at the nativity display. The donkey was gone, replaced by a mound of dust and chunks of stone.

'The donkey,' I whispered. 'I blew up the donkey.'

'You did. You really did! One minute it was there, the next it was like *Ka-boom*!' She was bobbing excitedly from foot to foot. 'How did you do it?'

'I don't know. I didn't mean to,' I replied. I hadn't meant to blow it up, but that didn't change the fact that I had. A shiver travelled the length of my spine.

'Are you OK?' Ameena asked.

I felt for the scratches the beast had dug into my back, but found none. 'Fine. I think I just had the weirdest dream,' I said, at last.

'I get that a lot,' Ameena nodded. 'One time I dreamt I was an egg. Just, like, a big egg, but with a face and arms and stuff. And bees kept chasing me. Big, angry bees. What do you think that means?'

'Run,' I hissed.

'I tried,' she shrugged, 'but it's not easy when you're a giant egg.'

'RUN!' I shouted, scrabbling to my feet. I caught hold of her arm and pulled her with me towards the exit, barely letting her feet touch the ground. At the far end of the church, a dark figure hung limply from the statue of the cross, arms outstretched in the classic crucifixion pose. As we fled, it raised its head, scowled, and spat at us through swollen, stitched-up lips.

Chapter Eleven

THE BOY IN BLUE

Where are we going?' demanded Ameena. This time she was the one having difficulty keeping up, and I could barely hear her over the sound of the wind and the rain. 'Why are we running?'

'It's him,' I cried. 'It's Mr Mumbles. He's found us!'

'What, *already*? I saw the way you hit him. No one could have got up from that so fast!'

'He's not human,' I reminded her.

'Don't start that again,' she yelled. 'You don't want to tell me who he is, fine, but don't play stupid games with me.'

'What, you accept I can make a statue explode, but not that he's not human?' I cried. 'I'm not playing games, and he did get up!' I took a left down a side street and heard

Ameena follow. 'He was there in the church.'

'Is... are you sure?'

'Of course I'm sure,' I snapped. 'I saw him, he was there.' I turned another corner and kept running, my lungs heaving against my ribs. 'We need to get help. We can't do this alone any more.'

'Help?' she echoed. 'You're kidding, right? Who's going to want to help us fight *that*?'

'Ho ho ho!' cried the officer on duty, as I flung open the doors of the tiny police station and tumbled inside. On his head he wore a shiny paper hat, and in his outstretched hand he held a bright red Christmas cracker. 'Merry Christ—'

'Someone's trying to kill us!' I blurted.

'Oh,' the policeman said. His shoulders sagged in disappointment. 'That's put a dampener on that then,' he sighed, setting the cracker down on the desk. 'Been waiting all day for someone to come in and pull that.'

I gaped up at him, not quite sure what to say. It was a

relief to find someone on duty, and I'd been hoping he might turn out to be a square-jawed hero type with bulging muscles. There were times when you really wanted a square jaw and bulging muscles on your side, and this was one such occasion. Unfortunately, the officer on duty was almost the exact opposite of what I'd hoped for.

Even with the party hat covering the top of his head, it was plain to see he was balding. He'd obviously decided to compensate by growing the thickest, bushiest moustache he could muster, which right now was coated in whipped cream. On the desk in front of him wavy lines of steam swirled into the air from a mug of hot chocolate.

He may have had a square jaw once, but his saggy chins were making it difficult to tell for sure. All in all he was around forty centimetres too short, twenty kilos too heavy, and thirty years too old to be the hero I'd hoped for. But beggars can't be choosers, and he was the only one I had.

'Sorry,' he smiled, turning his attention from the cracker. 'You were saying?'

'Someone's trying to kill us,' I repeated. I thought it best not to reveal that the person trying to kill us had once been a figment of my imagination. 'He's out there—'

'What, *us*?' he gasped, panic-stricken. 'You and me?'

'No! Not me and you.'

'Oh, thank God,' he sighed.

'Me and...' I began, turning and gesturing towards Ameena. Or, at least, towards the place Ameena should have been. Behind me there was only an empty entranceway. 'Where did she go?'

'Where did who go?'

'The girl. The girl I came in with. She was right behind me.'

The policeman frowned. 'I didn't see anyone,' he said. 'And I've been watching the door for a while, waiting for someone to...' He paused and picked up the cracker again. 'You sure you don't want to just...?'

'*Listen*,' I snapped, 'I was with a girl, and someone was trying to kill us. We were hiding in the church, but he found us, and so we ran away, and now she's gone! She was right there, but now she's gone.'

'Right,' the policeman said, solemnly. 'I understand. I get what you're saying.'

'Good.'

'You don't want to pull the cracker.'

I slammed my fist down on the desk in frustration. 'Of course I don't want to pull the cracker!'

'I know, that's what I just said!' he scowled. 'I mean, it's not like I'm asking much.'

At that, I threw up my arms and turned back towards the door.

'Where are you going?' the officer asked. 'I need to take a statement.'

'A statement?' I shouted. 'Didn't you listen to anything I said? There's a maniac out there and my friend could be dying right now.'

'Listen, I'm sure she's fine,' he said, in what he probably thought was a calming voice. If anything, it just annoyed me even more. 'What's her name?'

'Ameena.'

'That's an unusual one, isn't it?'

'*Who cares?*' I snapped, stunned that anyone this incompetent could get any job, much less such an important one. 'She saved my life tonight, and I'm not going to stand back and let her die because of it.'

We stood there for a few moments, looking at each other, unsure what to do next. The policeman seemed to be going through his options in his head, and for a second I thought I might have gone too far. Was shouting at a police officer an arrestable offence?

'Wait here,' he said at last. The paper hat was pulled reluctantly from his head and replaced by his standard issue cap. He emerged from behind the desk and nodded towards a tatty sofa. 'Take a seat and I'll go check it out. If there's anyone out there I'll find them.'

'Thanks,' I nodded, gratefully. Even though I was ready to go back out and look for Ameena, I was relieved not to have to.

'Merry bleeding Christmas,' I heard the officer mutter, before the door swung open and he was swallowed by the howling storm.

*

For several minutes, I stood by the window, trying to look out into the darkness. The glare of the lights turned the glass into a mirror, and all I could see was myself staring back. Freezing rain raged against the pane, shaking it in its frame. Mr Mumbles could be standing right outside, looking in, and I wouldn't know a thing about it.

Shivering, I turned away and took in the room. Aside from the desk – which looked more like a shop counter than an actual desk – and the sofa, there wasn't a lot in the place. A stack of leaflets here, a gaudy decoration there – it was depressingly bare, and no place to be spending Christmas. Suddenly I wished I'd helped the policeman pull his cracker. I told myself I'd do it when he came back.

My clothes were cold, wet, and sticking to my skin, so I didn't much fancy the idea of taking a seat. Instead I snuck a sip of the policeman's hot chocolate, and paced nervously up and down, waiting for him to return.

I'd just picked up the hot chocolate for another drink when I spotted the figure lurking behind the sofa. The mug shattered noisily as it slipped from my hand. Even before it had hit the floor, though, I realised my mistake.

'What are you doing down there?' I demanded. 'You nearly gave me a heart attack!'

'Sorry,' Ameena shrugged, unfolding herself upright. 'I don't have a very good relationship with the police. Probably should have warned you.'

'I thought Mr Mumbles had got you! I thought you'd been grabbed and—'

'I know,' she interrupted. 'I heard.' She looked me up and down and smiled. 'You were really going to run out there after me, huh?'

I felt my cheeks flush red. She'd heard everything! 'Suppose so,' I nodded.

She crossed to the window and cupped her hands against it so she could block the light and see outside. Why hadn't I thought of that?

'Anything?' I asked.

'Rain,' she replied. 'Lots and lots of — OH MY GOD, THERE HE IS!'

'Where?' I shrieked, jumping in fright. Ameena turned, a toothy grin almost splitting her face in two.

'I can't believe you fell for that twice.'

'Stop doing that!' I said, my heart rate still accelerating rapidly. 'It wasn't funny the first time.'

'Trust me, it was bloody hilarious *both* times. You should have seen your face,' she laughed. She was still giggling when she hopped up and sat on the front desk. 'It's been a while now. Aren't you going to ask?' she said, eventually.

'Ask what?'

'All the questions you've been dying to ask me. Who I am, where I'm from, why you've never seen me before. That stuff.'

'I hadn't thought about it,' I told her, even though I really had. 'To be honest I've had other things on my mind.'

'Now's the perfect time then,' she said. 'Danger's passed.'

'No it hasn't,' I argued. 'He's still out there!'

'Meaning we're safe in here for now.' She paused to let me think about this. It sounded almost too good to be true, but she might be right. 'So,' she continued, 'go ahead and ask me.'

'OK,' I shrugged, if only to shut her up. 'I know your name, but who are you?'

'No one in particular,' she answered, innocently. 'Next question.'

'What's the point?' I tutted, turning away. 'If I ask where you're from you'll only say "nowhere special" or something like that.'

'You're no fun,' she smirked. 'I'm from out of town,' she announced. 'Way out of town, actually. I'm moving into the house next to yours.'

'The Keller House?' I gasped, spinning back to face her. 'You're moving into the Keller House?'

'I didn't know that's what it's called, but if you say so.'

'Wow,' I whistled. 'You're braver than I thought.'

'I'm not even going to ask why you said that,' she winced. 'Anyway, I was taking a look around the house when I saw your little wrestling match with Mumbles. Thought you could use a hand. Conveniently, someone left a baseball bat lying around. You know the rest after that.'

'Why were you looking around on Christmas Day?'

'My family doesn't celebrate Christmas,' she said with a shrug.

'Is it against your religion or something?'

Ameena looked at me for a moment, then let out a long, loud laugh. Maybe it was just the sheer relief of being safe in the police station, but something about the way she laughed made me chuckle too. Before long we were both cackling like hyenas, with tears running down our cheeks.

'Against my religion,' she giggled. 'That's a good one.'

'Where are your family, anyway?' I asked.

'They're around,' she said. 'Why?' She was defensive now, not laughing.

'Just wondering,' I shrugged.

She looked at me, suspiciously. 'My mum and dad are going to follow me in a while.'

'Any brothers or sisters?'

'A brother.'

'Older or younger?'

'What's this about?' she demanded. 'How come you're so interested in my family all of a sudden?'

'I was only asking,' I protested. 'Just trying to take my mind off everything, that's all. Anyway, you're the one who wanted me to ask you questions.'

'Hmm,' she frowned. 'OK. What about you?'

'Just me and my mum,' I told her. 'And my nan, but she doesn't live with us.'

'Where's your dad?'

'Your guess is as good as mine,' I shrugged, beginning to wish I hadn't started the conversation.

'Oh,' Ameena said. 'I see. Sorry.' She looked down at the cracker on the desk beside her, thought for a moment, then picked it up. 'Here,' she said, offering me one end. 'Merry Christmas.'

'I don't think he'd want us to pull that,' I said, nervously. The policeman had seemed pretty attached to that cracker.

'Then we won't tell him,' she sighed. 'Come on, this'll be the first time I've ever done this. Chances like this don't come along very often for me, you know?'

I took the shiny red paper in my hand and gripped it

tightly. Ameena was almost bouncing up and down with excitement. 'You're a strange one,' I said.

'You don't know the half of it,' she smiled, and we both gave a short, sharp pull. I looked down and found myself holding the big end. 'No fair, you won!' she cried, but I could tell she wasn't really bothered. 'Let's see what you got.'

I tipped the torn cracker on to the desk, letting its contents spill out. They were less than impressive.

'That's got to be the smallest water pistol ever made,' said Ameena, as I picked up the tiny yellow gun. 'I could spit more than that holds.'

'Ooh look, lime green,' I smiled, unfolding a paper crown and slipping it on to my head. Almost at once it began to dissolve against my wet hair. 'Does it suit me?'

'It looks like someone blew their nose on your head,' she said. 'Which, if you ask me, isn't a bad look for you.'

'Well, thanks,' I grinned, picking up the last item. It was a small rectangle of paper. 'Ready for the joke?'

She pulled her legs up so they were crossed on the desk in front of her, and rested her chin on her hands. 'Go for it.'

'These are usually terrible, so you should probably brace yourself.'

'Braced and ready!'

'Right,' I began, but immediately stopped. I studied the writing on the paper, then turned it over to see if there was anything more written on the other side. Blank. I turned the paper back and read the text again. It made no sense.

'What does it say?'

I frowned and showed her the single word printed in thick, black type on the paper. She leaned forwards and read it aloud. 'Duck,' she said.

And at that, the doors exploded.

Chapter Twelve

THE GET AWAY

For the second time that night I shielded my face from flying shards of glass. Ameena tumbled backwards from the desk, crying out as a large, awkward shape tumbled through the air and hit the back wall with a thud.

I clambered over the desk, away from the gaping wound in the front wall, and fell clumsily to the floor. The limp body of the policeman lay next to me; bleeding all over, groaning in pain. I leaned down to try to help him, but a firm grip yanked me by the collar.

'Get up,' Ameena hissed, pulling me up on to my knees. 'Move!'

I scrambled after her, unable to tear my eyes from the barely breathing policeman. Only a low mumbling from the doorway was enough to get me to look away.

The metal frames were all that remained of the double doors, and even they were bent so far they'd torn free of the top hinges. The tall panes of glass which had filled the frames were now shattered and spread over the floor and desk.

My attention, though, was fixed on the figure standing just inside the room. A smile played at the edges of Mr Mumbles' mouth, stretching his stitches almost to breaking point. The pathway of glass cracked and crackled as he slowly began to advance.

'Come on, there's got to be a back door,' Ameena barked, grabbing me by the arm and shoving me hard into the corridor behind the desk. I watched in horror as she dropped to her knees and began to go through the policeman's pockets. He groaned, his eyes half open.

'*You're robbing him?*'

'I'm looking for keys!'

Already, Mr Mumbles was almost at the front desk. His dark, sunken eyes bored into me as he continued his steady approach.

'Hurry up!' I begged. 'He's coming!'

'Got them,' Ameena yelped. She sprung back up and we hurried along the short corridor until we found the back door of the station. Locked. Not for the first time, I was relieved Ameena was with me. Stopping for the keys would never have occurred to me. I'd have been trapped with nowhere to go.

She studied the lock and held up the hefty metal key ring. There were easily thirty keys hanging from it. This was going to take time – something we didn't have. Behind us, Mr Mumbles entered the corridor and strode slowly towards us, like an undertaker in a funeral procession. His low mumbling echoed and amplified between the narrow walls, until the sound seemed to be coming at us from every direction at once.

'What is it?' Ameena demanded. 'What's he saying?'

I shook my head. I couldn't make the words out properly. 'I don't... Something... something about ripping our eyes out.'

'Sorry I asked.'

The first key slipped easily into the lock, but didn't turn. The next few didn't even make it all the way in. Ameena slammed her shoulder against the wood in rage and frustration, but the door wouldn't budge. Mr Mumbles' footsteps *click-clacked* on the polished floor, louder and louder, closer and closer.

I focused, trying to summon up the strength I'd felt earlier. I could do this. I could break down this door.

THUMP! I swung with my right arm, striking the door with the heel of my hand, like I'd seen people do in kung fu movies. The door remained closed, but my wrist hurt like hell.

'Get it open!' I screamed, clutching my wounded arm.

'I'm trying!'

Click. Clack. Click. Clack. The footsteps drew closer. Another key jangled in the lock. Not the right one. *Click. Clack. Click. Clack.* He was almost on us now. Another few seconds and we'd be done for! *Click. Clack. Click. CLICK!*

Ameena cried out in triumph as the next key turned all the way. At once, the door was whipped wide open by the wind. We collided and almost fell over each other in our rush to get outside. I only managed to stay on my feet by catching on to the bonnet of the police car which sat, silent and alone, in the small station car park.

The indicator lights of the vehicle gave a sudden bright flash, as Ameena pressed a button on the largest of the keys. With a *bleep* and a *clunk*, the front two doors unlocked.

'Get in,' she urged, throwing open the driver's door and sliding in behind the steering wheel. I glanced up at the station in time to see Mr Mumbles step out after us. There was no time to lose.

'Can you drive?' I asked, as I leapt into the passenger seat and pulled the door closed. Ameena turned the key in the ignition and the engine roared into life.

'How hard can it be?' she shrugged, noisily grinding the gear stick into place. 'Hold on!'

My head was snapped almost to my chest as she slammed the accelerator down with her foot, sending the car speeding backwards. Something – maybe the tyres, maybe me – screeched sharply. Then, with a grinding of metal, the back end buckled against the wall of a neighbouring building.

'Wrong way!' I shouted. 'Forwards, go forwards!'

'I know that!' she snarled, crunching the gears and eyeing up the narrow exit out of the car park. From the corner of my eye I saw her face twist into a scowl, as Mr Mumbles stepped in front of us, blocking our escape.

She spoke, but whatever she said was lost beneath another scream – definitely from the tyres, this time. With a sudden jolt, the car lunged forwards. For a few seconds we weaved wildly as Ameena fought to get control of the wheel, and then we were going straight, and heading right for Mr Mumbles.

He wasn't smiling when the front of the car struck him. His body bent in half, smashing his head off the shiny white bonnet, before our momentum dragged him down and under the front wheels. Something below us gave a loud *crunch*. I felt my stomach spasm, and for a second I thought I was going to be sick.

'Got him!' cried Ameena. She braked hard. Another *crunch*, the sound of something ripping, and then the only noises were the low hum of the engine and our own unsteady breathing.

I looked across at Ameena. Her tan skin looked ashen white. Her body was shaking, her hands gripping tight on the wheel. I couldn't tell if she was laughing or crying.

'I got him,' she repeated, more quietly this time. 'I got him.'

'What do we do now?' I asked.

'I got him. I so got him.'

'Ameena?'

'Got him.' She was babbling now, tears streaking her face. 'Did you see that? I got him.'

'You did,' I said, softly. I was shaking, too, but somehow managing to hold myself together. Just. 'You got him. You saved us.'

'I did, didn't I?' she trembled. 'I had to do it, didn't I?'

Before I could open my mouth to reassure her, a powerful fist punched a hole straight through the back windscreen. We spun in our seats in time to see the entire safety glass window being ripped clear of its rubber seal. Mr Mumbles – his mouth still tightly shut – gave an animal roar of rage from deep down in his throat.

Without a word, Ameena forced the gear stick into reverse and powered the car backwards. Mr Mumbles' expression didn't change as we smashed him against the wall, pinning him in place. The abrupt stop bounced me against the seat, then threw me sharply forwards. I cried out in pain as my head thudded off the dashboard.

My fingers flew to the wound and came away red. Cut. I could worry about that later. Mr Mumbles' arms were stretched out, reaching into the car. His dirty, scarred fingers clawed at the air just a few centimetres from us.

We both pushed open our doors and rolled out, desperate to be as far from the monster as possible. For a few seconds we watched him, as he struggled to move his legs and get a grip on the ground. His feet were trapped under the car, and no matter how hard he tried to move them, they kept slipping from under him. Incredibly, he didn't look like he was hurt, but at least he was trapped. For now.

'W-what is he?' Ameena stammered. 'Why is he still moving?'

'I told you,' I said, as gently as I could, 'he's my imaginary friend. I don't know how, but he came back. Really came back.'

'SHUT UP! That's impossible,' she cut in. There was an uncertainty to her voice, though, as if she was finally starting to believe it. 'It's... it's impossible. He's just a guy. He's just a freaky guy!'

'You've seen what he can do,' I protested. 'The garage. This. You said yourself, no one could survive them. No one human, anyway. I'm telling the truth, Ameena. You've got to believe me.'

She shook her head. 'What I've got to do is get out of here,' she said. 'This isn't my fight. I shouldn't be involved in this. I've got to go.' She turned and sprinted off through the car park exit, leaping over the gate and rounding the corner before I could even start to give chase.

'Ameena!' I called after her, doing my best to catch up. 'Ameena, wait!'

I climbed over the entrance gate and ran out into the adjoining street. The wind whistled along it, bending trees and swirling discarded scraps of sparkly wrapping paper into the air.

Halfway across the road I stopped and squinted against the rain in both directions, but Ameena was nowhere to be seen. Mr Mumbles was stuck, but he'd get out sooner or later, *and Ameena was nowhere to be seen.*

I hurried back through the broken front door of the police station and ran up to the desk. The mosaic of blood-stained glass still lay on the floor, but the policeman was gone. Where was he? Had he woken up? Could he have somehow crawled away? No, he would have left a blood trail on the floor behind him if he had.

I searched through the other few rooms of the station, just in case he was hiding in there somewhere. I found no one. Wherever the policeman had gone, I was on my own.

Alone.

Just like I'd been in the house.

That was it! The house. Mr Mumbles had first turned up in the house, and that was where I'd found his picture too. If there was a way of stopping him for good, that was surely where I'd find it.

A jolt of fear travelled the length of my body, but there

was no way of escaping what I had to do next. There was nothing else for it. I had to go back.

I had to go back into the attic.

Chapter Thirteen

A NOTE FROM THE PAST

It took me almost ten minutes to make my way home, what with the wind and rain. They worked together, hammering into me and keeping me from running. I wasn't sure if I had enough energy left to run, anyway, so I spent most of the trek with my head down, only looking up to get my bearings now and again.

As I walked I went over the events of the last few hours. Too much had happened that night for me to get my head round it all, but maybe if I broke it up into smaller chunks I'd be able to make proper sense of it all.

The cracker had been a warning. But how was that possible? How could someone have known to tell me to 'duck'? It didn't make any sense, but then not much about tonight made much sense.

When I thought about the cracker my mind turned to thoughts of Mr Mumbles, creeping in through the broken doorway, dead eyes fixed on mine. I quickened my pace, suddenly convinced I was being followed. The weather made it hard going to keep up the faster speed, and I found myself slowing back down again almost immediately. There was no way Mr Mumbles was getting free of the wreckage any time soon, so I had no need to worry.

Sure, I thought. *Keep telling yourself that.*

There was no sign of Mum's car when I finally arrived at the house. I didn't know whether to be relieved or disappointed. I'd have felt safer with her around, but I couldn't stand the thought of putting her at risk. I wanted her to be as far away from the danger as possible. I only wished I could do the same myself, but if Mr Mumbles was going to be stopped, I would have to be the one to do it.

I glanced across at the Keller House, searching for any movement or sign of life inside. Nothing. Either Ameena wasn't there or she was lying low. I thought about going over to see if she was around, but decided against it. She was right, this wasn't her fight. She'd saved my life over and over again tonight, but she'd had enough, and I had no right dragging her back into my problems. Besides – stupid as it sounded – the idea of going into the Keller House terrified me more than the idea of going into the attic.

I took a deep, steadying breath and began walking in the direction of my front door. It still lay wide open, the house itself dark and silent. My legs tried to hesitate at the gate, but I forced them to keep walking. This was it, then.

I was going in.

The electricity was still off.

Fantastic. As if heading back to the attic wasn't bad enough, I had to do it in the dark.

I crept slowly up the stairs, the flickering candle in my hand my only source of light. Shadows flitted and scurried up the walls on either side, bending and warping as I passed. The wind whipped in through the broken living-room window and howled up the stairs, pushing me on like an invisible hand on my back.

At last I creaked my way to the landing. Below me, the darkened stairway opened wide. It looked almost like a giant, cavernous mouth getting ready to swallow me whole. *Great*, I thought. *Creep yourself out even more, why don't you?*

Pushing the image from my mind, I reached overhead and unclipped the flimsy catch of the attic trapdoor. The hatch swung free, and the familiar stench of damp rolled down from the dark confines of the attic.

Standing on tiptoes, I stretched my free arm up into the gloom. My hand found the ladder and I slowly eased it all the way down to the floor. I hesitated, my foot poised on the bottom rung, the candle held tightly in my trembling hand.

Despite the cold, I noticed a thin film of sweat spreading out across my forehead. This was crazy. I should be getting hold of the police up in the town, not clambering into the attic to look for clues! It was madness, if not suicide.

But no, if there was a way to stop Mr Mumbles for good

it'd be up there among the dust and the junk and the small, furry rodents. If I didn't stop him, I'd always be running, always be hiding, always be afraid. I had to go through with it.

Gritting my teeth and tightening still further my grip on the candle, I stepped on to the next rung, said a silent prayer to anyone who'd listen, and pulled myself up into the waiting darkness.

Nothing. For twenty minutes I searched through old boxes, ripped open plastic bags and generally tore the attic apart. Nothing. There was nothing up there which looked even vaguely capable of stopping a homicidal maniac, imagined or otherwise.

The most interesting thing I'd found was an envelope containing photos of Mum when she was younger. She was happy and smiling, like she didn't have a care in the world. I realised I'd never seen her looking quite like that before. Not that she was miserable or anything, I'd just never seen her looking quite *that* happy. I stuffed the photos into my pocket and made a note to ask her about them later. Assuming I lived that long.

I stood in the gloom, casting my eyes over the mess I'd caused. Good job no one came up here too often. Deflated, I sighed and felt my shoulders fall. I'd been sure this was where I'd find the answer, but there was nothing. The loft held nothing but old paperwork, baby clothes and boxes of toys.

Toys. Something about toys. A sleeping memory stirred at the back of my mind, then dozed off again. I screwed my eyes tight, trying to catch the thought before it disappeared for good. What was it about my old toys?

Tucked away in the corner was a large wooden box. It had once been painted white, but now was covered in hundreds of colourful doodles. Here and there I'd scratched my name into the paint. Though I couldn't remember scraping my name, I remembered the box. Even here, it made me feel strangely warm, as if it had absorbed all of my old happy memories, and was now letting them seep back out.

It had been one of the first things I'd looked in when I'd

clambered up into the attic. I don't know what I expected to find, but when I'd seen it was overflowing with die-cast cars, toy soldiers and plastic dinosaurs I'd left it alone. Now I went to it again, not sure what I was looking for, but certain the action figures and vehicles weren't it.

Searching through the box would take forever. Since I didn't have that long, I took hold of one side and pushed. The box was heavy, but with a couple of big shoves it tipped all the way over. A mass of Power Rangers, trains and balls of various shapes and sizes slid like an avalanche on to the bare wooden floor.

I dug into them, pushing and throwing them to the side one by one. They were all familiar, but not what I needed. Reaching into the box, I dragged more and more toys free. A roller skate. A teddy. A pirate hat. Wrong. All wrong. Not what I was looking for. There had to be something in here. There *had* to be!

My fingers brushed against rough material and I had to twist my hand to get a proper grip. It took three pulls to dislodge the thing from the bottom of the box, where two tanks and a transforming helicopter had it tightly trapped.

It was a bag. An old school bag by the look of it. A full one, too. I had just turned it over in my hands, hunting for the zip that would open it, when I spotted the note. It wasn't easy to miss, being written on an A4 piece of paper and taped directly over the mouth of the bag.

Written on the note in big, childish, red crayon letters were the words:

in case of

emergunsy

And below the writing, in thick, black crayon, was the outline of a man in a hat and a long flowing coat. An outline that had been warped and distorted in the years since then, but which was still familiar.

Mr Mumbles.

My heart skipped a beat. I knew then that I'd found it. I'd found the thing that would stop him.

I set my candle down on the floor, ripped the note off the bag and yanked on the zip. It moved stiffly, but I managed

176

to wrestle it open. Apprehensively, I reached inside and pulled out the first thing I found.

For a long time I knelt there, staring at the worn rubber suction cup of the plastic arrow, not sure how to react. The bag held four or five of the arrows, along with a tiny toy bow, just like in the drawing I'd discovered earlier. There was a short sword in there, too. It was just as plastic as the bow and the arrows, and just as useless. Maybe they could hurt the Mr Mumbles of my five-year-old imagination, but this one was real, and plastic weapons weren't going to stop someone who'd survived being run over by a car. Twice.

'Useless,' I hissed, snatching up as many of the toys as I could hold in both hands. 'It's all *useless*.'

I quickly stood up, arms raised, ready to hurl the plastic junk across the attic. The bag had been my last hope – my *only* hope – and it had turned out to be just another dead end.

I snapped my arms forwards, throwing the things as hard and as fast as I could. Or trying to, at least. But as I threw, my fingers refused to open. The play weapons stayed right where they were in my hands.

Again I tried to lob them. Again my grip didn't budge. A third attempt ended the same way. Try as I might, I couldn't throw the toys away.

I looked down at my hands. They were holding on to the toys so tightly my knuckles were white. I had wanted to get rid of them, but some part of me refused to let go. Something deep in my subconscious mind was making sure I held on to the contents of the bag.

Shaken, I stuffed the toys back in the satchel and swung one strap over my shoulder. If my subconscious was so determined to keep it around then maybe the bag *would* come in handy. OK, I couldn't see how, but it might. Stranger things had happened today, and I'd been slap bang in the middle of most of them.

The tiny flame flickered in irritation as I picked up the candle and took one final look around the attic, hoping to spot some other clue to defeating my former friend. I knew in my heart, though, that there was nothing else to find.

There was no magic wand I could wave to make Mr Mumbles go away. I would have to find some other way to stop him. Whatever it took.

I made my way back to the hatch, and was just about to step on to the ladder when I heard it: A slow, regular *thud, thud, thud* from down below. I sucked in my breath and leaned back away from the hole in the floor. I didn't want to make any noise, so I squeezed the flame of the candle out between two fingers – something I'd always thought looked cool, but which I'd always been too scared to try in the past.

It wasn't cool. It bloody hurt.

But burnt fingertips didn't seem like anything worth worrying about now. Instead I could concern myself with the fact that someone was in the house.

And they were coming up the stairs.

In the blackness I waited, unable to move for fear of drawing attention to myself. My breathing sounded louder than the gales outside. My heart thudded with more force than the rain on the sloping roof above my head. Already I could feel my legs wobbling. Any minute now they'd give up on me completely. Any minute after that, I'd be dead.

Thud, thud, thud. The footsteps were almost right beneath me now. Next I'd hear the creaking of the metal ladder, and then that ugly head of his would appear through the hatch. Since there was no other way out of the attic, I'd be trapped.

There'd be no escaping this time.

Chapter Fourteen

REVELATIONS

The thudding stopped at the top of the stairs. Aside from the weather outside, there was nothing but silence in the house. I held my breath until it felt as if my lungs were about to go pop. Just a few seconds before they did, the quiet was shattered.

'Coo-ee!' called a familiar voice. 'You up there, Kyle?'

'Nan!' I cried, leaning over the hatch and peering down into the gloom. Her wrinkled face gazed up at me, illuminated by a candle of her own. Right at that moment, she was the most beautiful sight I'd ever seen. 'Nan, what are you doing here?' I half climbed, half jumped down the ladder, and gave her a grateful hug.

'The way was blocked,' she explained. 'A tree's on the

road.' Her grey eyebrows furrowed as she thought about this for a second. 'Or something like that.'

She was wringing her wrinkled hands together, obviously worried. 'I hope Albert's all right.' Her eyes were distant again, like a barrier had come up behind them. 'Poor Albert. I've got such a feeling something terrible's happened.' A single tear rolled down her wrinkled cheek. 'Oh, Albert!'

'Nan?' I kept my voice soft so as not to startle her. 'Nan, are you OK?'

Her eyes seemed to swim for a moment, as if they were trying to focus. When they finally found me I saw their usual sparkle was back. 'Stuck there for ages, we were,' she smiled, 'but your mum managed to get us turned round in the end.'

I smiled, glad to have the real Nan back so quickly. 'That's good. Is Mum with you?'

'Course she is, sweetheart. She's downstairs. Fixing the lights.'

I wanted to jump for joy. Even though I hadn't wanted Mum in danger, it was a relief to hear she was near. She'd know what to do. She'd sort it all out. She always did.

'We tried phoning the police station to find out what was happening. With the road, like.'

'The policeman's been hurt. Maybe killed,' I said, stopping short of any other explanation. Saying it out loud made my body shake and my mouth go dry. Hot tears sprung up behind my eyes. The policeman could be dead. Properly dead.

'Oh,' Nan nodded, matter-of-fact. 'That'll be why he wasn't answering, then.'

We both jumped as the electricity suddenly clicked back on, flooding the house with light. A few seconds later, Mum appeared at the bottom of the stairs, her cheeks flushed red from the cold.

'Mum!' I jumped down the first few steps. 'You're here!'

'Kyle,' she gasped, moving up to meet me halfway, 'what happened to your head?' I winced as she gently touched the cut on my forehead. I'd completely forgotten about it, but now she'd mentioned it I could feel it throbbing away. I saw the concern in her eyes and everything I'd been holding back all night burst free all at once.

'Mum, I'm sorry I got cut and wrecked everything but it wasn't my fault I had to get out he was after me and he kept coming he kept coming and the policeman... the policeman got hurt and that's my fault because I shouldn't have gone there and now he's going to come after me again and he's going to get me.' I was babbling uncontrollably, unable to hold back my emotions.

'Wait, wait, slow down,' Mum comforted. 'The policeman's coming to get you?'

'No,' I said, my voice a hoarse whisper, 'not the policeman.'

'Who then?'

I wiped my tears away and looked her right in the eye. 'Mr Mumbles,' I whispered. 'Mr Mumbles is coming to get me.'

Mum stared back at me, her jaw slack. She didn't say anything for what felt like forever. Her eyes darted across to Nan, then back to me.

'What did you say?' she asked in a low whisper. Her eyes looked hard, like a defensive wall had come up behind them.

'Mr Mumbles,' I repeated. 'He's come back. He wants to kill me.'

Mum stepped back and covered her mouth with her hand. It trembled slightly as she held it there, no longer looking at me.

'Kyle,' she spoke flatly, 'Mr Mumbles isn't real. We've been through all this.'

'He is,' I insisted.

'Don't do this to me, Kyle.' Her eyes were pleading now. 'Don't do this. Not again.'

'He's real! He is!' A thought suddenly struck me. 'The window!' I exclaimed, ducking past her and running down the stairs. 'He broke the window, come see.'

I stumbled into the living room and skidded to a stop. Mum appeared quickly behind me, with Nan eventually joining us several seconds later. I shook my head in disbelief as I checked over the window.

'It was broken,' I protested, running my fingers over the

ice-cold pane. 'There was glass all over the floor!'

'It looks all right now, sweetheart,' Nan said, softly. 'Maybe you imagined it.'

'You don't just imagine a psycho with stitched-up lips crashing through your living-room window!' I snapped. 'He was here. I tried to escape, but he was strangling me and—'

'That's enough,' said Mum, sternly.

'And a girl saved me,' I continued. 'Her family have bought the Keller House and are going to move in, and she saw me—'

'No one's bought the Keller House,' Mum dismissed. 'I'd have heard about it.'

'But the policeman! What about the policeman? At the station. He was hurt.'

Mum jolted forwards as if there were pins beneath her feet.

'I'll call the station in town and find out if anything happened,' she announced, curtly. 'Where's the phone?'

'I dropped it—' I started to say, but I stopped when Mum lifted the handset from the top of the TV.

'Must've picked itself up again,' she said. I watched her punch in a short series of numbers. She kept her eyes on me as she held the phone to her ear and waited.

'Ah yes, hello,' she said, when someone finally answered. 'I wonder if you can help me. I'm calling from Kincraggie village. I'd heard the officer on duty tonight was involved in some kind of accident, and I wanted to check if—'

The person on the other end interrupted. Mum's eyebrows raised. She nodded, slowly. 'I see. No, that's fine. Not to worry. Thanks for your help.'

The phone gave a faint *beep* when Mum slid it back down into the cradle.

'Well?' I asked.

'There was no one on duty in the village station,' Mum said. 'It's been locked up all day.'

'What? No!' I protested. 'There was someone there. I saw him. I spoke to him! He went out looking for Mr Mumbles, but he got hurt.'

'So where is he now?' Mum asked.

'He...' I hesitated. Where *had* the policeman gone? One

minute he was groaning on the ground, the next he was gone. 'He just kind of disappeared,' I said.

'Kyle,' Mum said, her voice softer now. She leaned forwards and took hold of my shoulders. 'I don't know what you think you saw, but trust me, there's no such thing as Mr Mumbles. When you were young you imagined him, but then we... then you... then he went away. You stopped imagining him. You forgot about him.'

'So what are you trying to say?,' I sneered, pulling away. 'I've hallucinated the whole thing, have I? It's all just been my imagination playing tricks on me, has it?'

'Well, it wouldn't be the first time!' Mum snapped. She immediately leaned back, biting on her lip. Anxiety flitted across her face before she forced a smile and began to make a move towards the kitchen. 'Now,' she sang, 'who fancies a cup of tea?'

'What do you mean, "it wouldn't be the first time"?' I asked. 'Has something like this happened before?'

'Hmm? Oh, no, forget I said anything,' she beamed. 'How about some hot chocolate? I think I've got some—'

'You should tell him, Fiona,' Nan said. Her voice was sober. The wrinkles on her face were deep with worry. 'He deserves to know.'

'Know what?' I demanded. 'What should I know?'

Mum paused in the doorway, her back still to me. She inhaled deeply, and let out a long, quiet sigh. When she turned round, her cheeks were wet with tears.

'What do you remember,' she began, 'about the Keller House?'

The Keller House had been known as the Keller House for as long as I could recall, and not without good reason. There were various legends which circulated about how the house got its name, but they all boiled down to one thing: something terrible had happened within those walls, and it had happened to Mr Keller.

The stories were all slightly different. Mr Keller had been murdered by an intruder. Mr Keller had set himself on fire and burned alive. Mr Keller had died of a heart attack, then been eaten by his dogs. Whatever version of the tale you chose to believe, it always had an unhappy ending for poor Mr Keller.

Since then – and probably because of the stories – no one would move into the house. And so there it had stood, right next to ours, rotting and decaying over the years as the legends became more and more extravagant. The last one I'd heard had claimed Mr Keller had been doing experiments on deformed children, and they'd broken free and killed him, but most people found that hard to believe. Mr Keller was a solicitor, not a scientist.

Or he may have been a taxi driver, depending on who you believed.

'He was a retired businessman,' Mum corrected, once I had filled her in on the various versions of events I'd heard. 'Owned a few shops when he was younger, I think.'

The three of us were sitting on the couch now; me in the middle, Mum and Nan sandwiching me on either side. 'Sold everything up before moving here,' she continued. 'Just after you were born.'

'Was he murdered?' I asked. 'Did his dog eat him?'

'No, nothing like that.'

'Well, what then?'

Mum looked across at Nan, then swallowed hard. 'There was an accident in his swimming pool. A bad one. Someone... someone drowned. They died.'

'Mr Keller?' I asked.

'No, not Mr Keller.'

'Well, who then?'

Mum rested her hands on top of mine. Her expression was one I'd never seen before. 'You, Kyle,' she said. 'It was you.'

I blinked. My eyes darted over Mum's face, looking for some flicker there that would tell me she was kidding.

'But... but I'm not dead.'

'You were. For a minute or so. Mr Keller found you; pulled you out and gave you mouth-to-mouth. He brought you back. He saved you.'

I shook my head, hardly able to believe what I was hearing. 'How did it happen?' I asked.

Mum glanced over my shoulder at Nan. I heard her make

some small movement – a nod, maybe.

'You said it was *his* fault,' Mum said, her voice choked with emotion. 'You said it was Mr Mumbles. Told us he tried to kill you. It was a shock, because you hadn't mentioned him for a while before that. We thought you'd forgotten about him. *Hoped* you'd forgotten about him.'

And suddenly there it was again – that stirring in the darkest corners of my mind, as something struggled to come to the surface. Something I'd kept locked up back there for years. A memory I'd tried so hard to forget.

But not hard enough.

I am five. Five-and-a-half, maybe. In the front garden. Shivering. Breeze cold on my bare skin. Arm bands squeezing tight around my arms.

Running. Running in my trunks. Mum walking behind. Far behind. Grass squidging between my toes. Laughing. Arm bands like big muscles. I am Superman. I am the Hulk!

Don't bother to knock on the door. Never bother to knock.

Knows I'm coming. Push it open and run for the water. Want to jump and splash and play!

Mr Mumbles stands by the pool – good old Mr Mumbles, my best friend. Haven't played with him in a long time. Nearly forgot him. When I see him there I am happy. I laugh.

He doesn't.

His big hand scurries through my hair like Eensy Weensy Spider. He pulls, tighter and tighter, making me cry and scream; drags me to the edge. I am still crying as he forces me below the surface. Still crying as the water swirls into me. Still crying until the world goes dark and my head goes light and I can't cry any more, not even if I wanted to.

'I remember,' I gasped. 'The pool. I remember. That's why I'm scared of water, isn't it?'

'You never went swimming again,' Mum nodded. 'Mr Keller came through and found you floating there. He pulled you out and brought you back.' Tears rolled down her cheeks. 'Oh, God, Kyle, I thought I'd lost you.'

'What happened to Mr Keller?' I asked.

'What?' Mum looked surprised that I was even asking. She looked up at Nan.

'No idea,' Nan said with a shrug.

'He moved on again a little while after,' Mum said. 'I'm not sure where. The accident shook him up quite badly.'

'It wasn't an accident,' I said. 'It was Mr Mumbles.'

'That's what you kept saying at the time,' Mum nodded. 'But it *was* just an accident, Kyle. You slipped and fell into the pool.'

Angrily, I pulled my hands away from under hers and stood up. I crossed to the window and gazed out at the storm. For the first time, I noticed the CD player was back on the table and completely intact. Another of tonight's mysteries.

'Tell me about him,' I said.

'Mr Keller?'

'Mr Mumbles.' I turned back to the couch and looked down at Mum. 'When did he appear?'

She scowled and leaned back on the couch. 'I don't think this is—'

'Please,' I urged. 'I have to know.'

Mum tilted her head towards the ceiling and closed both

eyes. She sat like that for a few long moments, deep in thought. Finally, just as I was about to prompt her again, she started to speak.

'You were three, going on four,' she began. 'You'd been in playgroup a few months but... I don't know, you weren't really settling in.' She shook her head and opened her eyes. 'We shouldn't be going over this.'

'*Mum*,' I begged. 'Go on.'

'Right. Fine,' she said with a sigh. Her eyes were distant – unfocused – as she blew the dust off the pictures in her head. 'You didn't like it because the other kids... some of the others there, they couldn't understand you properly.'

I frowned. 'How come?'

'Speech problems,' said Mum.

'You were a terrible lazy speaker,' Nan chimed in. 'A real mumbler. Like you were talking with a mouth full of custard sometimes.'

'I could understand you fine,' Mum was quick to point out. 'I didn't notice a problem at all, but apparently everyone else did.'

Suddenly everything made perfect sense. 'And so I dreamed up an invisible friend with the same problem as me! That's when I started seeing him.'

'Pretty much,' Mum nodded. 'The doctor said it was harmless. It was your way of trying to deal with the problems you were having. He said it'd pass soon enough.' She glanced away as she recalled a visibly painful memory. 'But it didn't. It got worse.'

'In what way?'

'You started taking him with you everywhere. You'd talk about him all the time. And I mean *all* the time. Mr Mumbles did this, Mr Mumbles did that.'

'I didn't see it as a big problem,' Nan told me.

'Maybe it wasn't,' Mum admitted. 'Not then. Not until you started the speech therapy.'

'What happened?'

'He changed, you said. Became angry and started to scare you. I'd hear you screaming in the night and you'd say Mr Mumbles had come through your window. You'd say he was going to hurt you if you kept going to the sessions.'

'You were nearly five then,' Nan added. 'About to start school. We didn't know what to do. At our wits' end, we were.'

'We got you help,' said Mum. 'Professional help.'

'What, like a psychiatrist?' I gasped.

'A psychologist. A child psychologist. They tried to help you get rid of him.'

'Did it work?'

Mum shook her head. 'Got worse again, if anything.'

'So what happened?' I demanded. 'How did I get rid of him?'

'It was your nan's idea in the end. She thought that if your imagination was strong enough to make him so real to you – so vivid – then your imagination was strong enough to send him away.'

'You kicked his backside!' Nan grinned, triumphantly. 'In your imagination,' she added, after Mum frowned at her.

'We don't know exactly what happened,' Mum continued. 'But after Nan convinced you that you were the only one who could send him away, you asked me to help you up into the attic, and to leave you there for half an hour. I wasn't sure about it, but... well, we didn't know what else to do. After that half hour you came back down. You never spoke about Mr Mumbles again.'

'But all that was different,' I argued. 'I was a kid then. This isn't like that!'

'He was *real* to you, Kyle,' answered Mum. 'You saw him as clearly as you saw anyone else. But he wasn't real. He was in your head. It was all just in your head.'

She stood up from the couch and joined me by the window. The backs of her fingers felt soft as she gently stroked my cheek. 'Just like it is now.'

I opened my mouth to speak, but no words sprung immediately to mind. I glanced behind me at the CD player and the window. They were both still undamaged and intact.

Could she be right? It seemed impossible, but then it didn't seem nearly as impossible as my childhood invisible friend coming to life. Besides, my visit to the Darkest Corners had seemed real, but that had been just some bizarre nightmare. What if Mum *was* right? What if I was losing my mind?

What if I really *had* imagined the entire thing?

Chapter Fifteen

THE TRUTH

I sat there on the couch, in front of the window that wasn't broken, and which possibly never had been. My head was in my hands, my eyes fixed on the floor, as I tried to make sense of the world.

Was I going mad? Was that it? I'd seen Mr Mumbles – touched him – so if he wasn't real then what explanation was there, other than a complete mental breakdown?

I'd checked the kitchen, but the table and chair were no longer wedged against the back door. Instead, they sat where they always sat, and showed no signs of having been moved.

Mum was through in the kitchen now, and I could hear her filling the kettle. She seemed to think a cup of tea and a chat was all it was going to take to fix things, but I knew she was wrong. Whether Mr Mumbles was real or not, a cuppa wasn't going to solve anything.

I raised my head and glanced out of the window. The storm still raged as violently as ever. Through the rain, I could just make out the outline of the Keller House. Was Ameena there? In fact, was she even *real*? She had seemed out of place – larger than life, somehow – but for some reason, the idea of her not actually existing frightened me as much as Mr Mumbles ever had.

'Of course, she blamed your dad as well.'

I swivelled round and looked across at Nan. She was sitting in her usual armchair, working away on a crossword from yesterday's newspaper and sucking frantically on a boiled sweet as if it was the only thing keeping her alive.

'Fictional detective. Sherlock blank. Six letters,' she muttered.

'What did you say?'

'Fictional detective. Sherlock blank...' She grinned broadly and I could hear the sweet rattling against her teeth. She began to write on the page. 'Poirot. Sherlock Poirot, the little bald fella with the violin. Now,' she mused, tilting her head back so she could see through the reading glasses perched on the end of her nose, 'six down.'

'No, about my dad,' I said, quietly so as not to let Mum hear. 'What were you saying about my dad?'

'Hmm? Oh, nothing, nothing. Forget it, sweetheart.'

'Nan,' I said, imploringly. 'Please.'

She looked at me over the top of the glasses for a long time, not saying anything. At last, she folded the newspaper on to her lap, glanced across to the door, and began to speak.

'It's not important,' she said. She was keeping her voice low, so as not to let Mum hear. Nan knew Dad was a forbidden topic when I was around. 'I was just saying that your mum, she blamed your dad, too. For your... for the problems you were having. Thought maybe Mr Mumbles was a kind of replacement for him. A whatcha-ma-call-it. Father figure. What with him having run out on you both.'

I could hear Mum still busy in the kitchen, so I crept across and sat on the seat next to Nan's. A million questions raced through my head.

'What was he like?' I asked, trying to keep my voice level, despite my rising excitement. 'My dad.'

'Nice enough, I think,' Nan shrugged. 'He certainly made your mum a lot happier. Between you and me, she was a right miserable cow before he came along. No friends. Never went out. After she met him though... well, I've never really seen her smile like that before.' Nan reached across and patted me on the arm. 'Not until you came along, of course.'

I nodded. I'd always suspected Dad was a good guy, despite Mum's reaction whenever I asked about him. Still, it was nice to have it confirmed, especially by someone who was fully entitled to hate him.

'What did he look like?' I pressed.

'Oh, don't ask me, sweetheart. I never met him.'

'*What?*' I frowned. 'But you just said he was nice.'

'I said I *thought* he was nice, from the way he brightened your mother's face up. God knows she needed it.' Nan put down her pen and removed her glasses. 'He was supposed to come round a few times, but there was always something came up and he couldn't make it. As far as I know no one but your mum ever met him. No one I knew, anyway. I almost started to believe she was making him up at one point! But then *you* came along, and, well, you can't argue with evidence like that.'

'What about pictures?' I urged, feeling my spirits start to sink. 'You must have seen pictures of him?'

'Don't think so,' replied Nan, shaking her head. 'I'd have remembered if I had.'

'Are you sure?' I asked, as tactfully as I could. 'You know with… with your memory playing tricks on you sometimes.'

She breathed on the lenses of her glasses and began cleaning them on her cardigan. 'Some things I remember just fine,' she said. 'And I remember I never saw any photographs.'

Photographs. I suddenly remembered the ones from the attic. They were still in my pocket. My hands were shaking as I pulled them out and flipped through them. Mum. Mum. Mum. They all showed Mum on her own, smiling and happy, just like Nan had said. Mum at the park. Outside the cinema. In a café.

In some of them she held her arm up in a strange way. It was raised up to shoulder level, and sticking out to the side, like she was doing "I'm a Little Teapot" but had forgotten to mime the handle. I'd half noticed it earlier, but was now seeing it properly for the first time. It almost looked like she was...

Hurriedly I flipped back through the pictures until I came to the shot in the café. Something about it had seemed wrong. Out of place. I studied it now, searching for the answer.

Like all the pictures, this one was a self-portrait, taken at arm's length. You could see the arm that was holding the camera, and part of her head had been cut off. There was no mistaking it was Mum, though. There was also no mistaking the large glass of milkshake sitting on the table right in front of her.

One glass.

But two straws.

'How many people do you see in this picture?' I demanded, exploding into kitchen. Mum whipped round and reacted with horror at the sight of the café photo.

'Where did you get that?' she barked. 'How did you find it?'

'Just tell me how many you see!'

'You shouldn't be digging around in my private stuff, Kyle,' she barked, her face contorted in shock and anger. She sprung forward and whipped the photo from my hand. 'How many times do I have to tell you?'

'Mum, please,' I begged. 'How many people?'

'Two, of course!' she yelled. 'Now where did you get them?'

I heard nothing she said after that first word. The room spun and the floor turned to quicksand beneath me. *No.* It was impossible!

I held up another photo – Mum in the park this time. Alone.

'And this one?' I whispered. 'I want you to look really hard. How many people?'

'Two,' she said again, throwing her hands in the air. 'Why are you asking? Where did you get them?'

I turned the photo over and studied it. There was Mum doing 'I'm a Little Teapot'. There wasn't another soul in the picture. Not that I could see, at least.

'You have your arm round him,' I realised. 'That's what you're doing. Only I can't see him.'

'What? Look, what's this about?' she asked. Her voice was softer now, like she was about to start crying again.

'I have no idea,' I mumbled. I felt a strange, tightness creep across my stomach. There was only one explanation for the photos. Only one way to explain why Mum could see another person in them, but I couldn't. It was crazy, but it was the only solution.

I was looking at photographs of Mum and her invisible friend.

My dad.

But if that was the case, then that meant maybe I wasn't

losing my mind. That meant that maybe—

Rat-a-tat-tat.

'Oh, who's that at this time?' called Nan from the living room. 'I'll get it!'

'Wait, stop!' I hurled myself out of the kitchen, suddenly realising that I recognised that knock. I knew exactly who was on the other side of the door, waiting to pounce. 'Don't open it! It's him. It's Mr Mumbles!'

Mum burst through from the kitchen behind me. Her eyes were still red and puffy from crying. She looked tired and sad and angry and disappointed and everything bad in between.

'I thought we'd done this,' she sighed, marching straight for the front door. I stood in her path, trying to block the way, but she simply pushed past. 'I'm going to prove to you, Kyle, OK? I'm going to open this door and show you there's no such thing as...'

Her voice trailed off as she flung open the front door. A dark figure in a long coat lurked in the doorway. The rain pushed the brim of his hat down over his eyes, concealing them. The light of the house spilled out into the night, illuminating the crude, filthy stitches covering the monster's mouth.

'*My God*,' Mum gasped. 'But no. No, it can't...'

I dragged her aside and slammed the door shut, only to find it blocked by Mr Mumbles' outstretched arm. Again and again I tried to force it closed, tried to force him out, but the arm remained there, unflinching.

Desperately I raised my foot and kicked his hand, crushing it against the door frame. It didn't move. I kicked out again, harder this time, and heard the wooden door frame give a crack. Still, he held on. As I fired a third kick at him, his fingers twisted and caught me by the ankle. Frantically, I began to hop, trying to keep my balance.

Mum screamed as the door was thrown open. Mr Mumbles yanked on my leg, sending me staggering sideways. I threw my hands out, clutching at anything I could as I tried to stay standing. My fingers found the curtains, but they weren't enough. The curtain rail tore from the wall as I crashed to the floor.

Mr Mumbles gave my leg a sharp, sudden twist, and I felt a cry of pain escape my lips as something in my hip went *pop*. I kicked out with my free foot, exactly as I'd done during our first encounter tonight. Once again, my blows had no effect. His sunken eyes fixed on me, years of hatred burning behind them. How could I fight something like this? He was a monster. Relentless and unstoppable.

No, that wasn't true, I realised. Something had stopped him once before! My eyes fell on the dusty old school bag that I'd left lying at the bottom of the stairs. *In case of emergunsy.* If I could just get free; just reach the bag...

Mum dived at Mr Mumbles, only to be sent sprawling by a vicious punch. I watched her spin round and round like a ballerina, before she crashed into the TV. It hit the ground at the same time as she did.

'Mum!' I cried. She wasn't moving. I could see blood on the carpet. Blood, like Ameena's blood, like the policeman's blood, and she wasn't moving. Why wasn't she moving? *'Mum!'*

And then he was on me, pinning me down again, blocking Mum from my view. I struggled uselessly against his strength, twisting and wriggling as I fought to be free. He was too strong. No matter how hard I fought, he was too strong.

CRASH! Mr Mumbles hissed with rage as Mum's best crystal vase smashed across the back of his head.

'Get your damn hands off my grandson,' Nan growled. Mr Mumbles looked up as she slammed our metal wastepaper bin down. It covered his head, blinding him. As he reached to remove it I dragged myself free and pulled myself to my feet.

'Help Mum,' I barked. She was still on the floor. Still bleeding. Still not moving. 'Look after her until I get back.'

'Where are you going, Kyle? What are you going to do?' Nan fretted. I snatched up my childhood schoolbag then stepped in front of Nan, protectively. Mr Mumbles let the bin slip to the floor and drew himself up to his full height.

'Years ago, you said that only I could stop him. I think you were right,' I explained, not taking my eyes off the nightmare standing before me. 'And I've finally figured out how to do it,' I said, my face set in an expression of grim determination. 'I finally know how to end this thing, once and for all!'

Chapter Sixteen

WHERE IT ALL BEGAN

The grass at my feet had been churned into mud by the driving rain. I slipped and slid as I ran across it, limping, my imaginary friend somewhere close behind. Ducking past him and getting him to follow me out of the house had been the hard part. The *really* hard part – that was still to come.

Wild winds wailed at me, whipping at my clothes, slowing me down. I pushed through them, my eyes fixed straight ahead on my destination. As if on cue a bolt of lightning ripped across the sky, and for a split second the Keller House lit up like a firework before me.

My hands caught the top of the fence separating the two gardens, and I threw myself over. The grass on the other side was long and thick. It tangled around my feet as I ran, like a million grabbing hands, reminding me of the forest from my nightmare in the church. I kicked through it and focused on what I was about to do. What I *had* to do – no longer just for my sake, but for my family's too.

When I was close to the house I risked a backwards glance. The driving downpour made it difficult to see, but I could pick out the shape of Mr Mumbles. He was this side of the fence, movingly slowly, like he had all the time in the world. Boy, did I have a surprise in store for him!

The wooden door practically crumbled as soon as I put my shoulder to it. I swallowed hard, fighting back an almost overwhelming urge to turn from this place and run. Years of suppressed terror bubbled to the surface as I stepped over the threshold, and into the place where Mr Mumbles had first tried to kill me.

Why had I come here? I wasn't completely sure. Partly it was because I wanted to draw him away from Mum and Nan. More than that, though, I could think of no better place for our final battle. He'd lain in wait for me here when I was five, preparing to kill me. Now it was time to turn the tables.

Cracked and wet rubber tiles squeaked underfoot as I crossed to the edge of the pool. At any other time it would be nothing more than a big rectangular hole in the floor, but weeks of rain pouring in through a dozen or more holes in the roof had almost filled the thing to the top. The water was dirty and dank, full of dark shapes and darker memories I'd give anything to forget.

I backed away and hid down in the shadows by the door, waiting. As I squeezed myself against the wall something pressed against my back. I turned and studied it. It was a life ring, tied with a long rope to a bracket on the wall.

I set my old school bag down on the tiles, then slipped the life ring over my head and pushed it down to my waist. The orange plastic had been stained shades of brown by years of neglect, but it seemed sturdy enough. I wasn't planning on going near the water, *but just in case*, I told myself. *Just in case.*

Reaching into my bag, I pulled out the tiny plastic bow and one arrow, then zipped the bag tight shut again and slung it back over my shoulders. The toys still felt pathetic and flimsy in my grip, but I tried not to think about that. They had worked before – I had *made* them work before – and I was staking everything on them working now too.

The light in the garage. The axe. The shield. I had done that, I was sure of it. Somehow I made it happen. And if I had – if I could do that - I could do anything.

Silently, I notched one of the arrows against the thin string of the bow, took aim at a space a pace or two inside the door, and waited.

Lightning danced across the sky and turned the next few seconds into a series of freeze-frame images. I felt cut off from my body, like an onlooker inside my own head, as the door was thrown wide open.

I saw the hulking shape of Mr Mumbles step through, watched my fingers release their grip on the string, heard the *boing* and followed the arc of the arrow as it whizzed in agonising slow motion through the air towards its target.

The arrow struck him on the arm. I watched the rubber tip thud against his coat, followed by the thin plastic rod as it rebounded harmlessly off. A second later, the arrow clattered on the tiled floor. A second after that, the world lurched back into full throttle.

With a throaty roar, Mr Mumbles turned and leapt for me. His fingers were in my hair before I could react, yanking so hard I thought my scalp would be ripped in two. I hurled my body weight against him as he dragged me over to the pool. It must've caught him off guard and knocked his balance, because almost at once he began to stumble.

Still holding me by the hair, he slipped on the tiles and we both tumbled down into the pool.

Freezing water stabbed at me as we crashed below the surface, sending shockwaves through my whole body. *So cold*. Hadn't been ready for the cold. It forced me to gasp, to open my mouth, and I spluttered as the murky grey liquid seeped down my throat.

The plastic ring bobbed me back up and I coughed up most of what I'd swallowed. The cold was overwhelming. It filled every thought – a pain like nothing I've ever known.

I still held the plastic bow in my hand. This had been a stupid idea. Stupid. Stupid. *Stupid*. I thrashed in the water, but my limbs were already beginning to go stiff. Fingers burning with cold now. Breathing impossible. Stupid. So cold. Had to get out.

My hands didn't feel like they were connected to the rest of me, but with some effort, I got them to follow orders. Trembling, and with the toy bow hooked by its string over my wrist, I took hold of the rope which tethered me to the wall. My muscles spasmed in protest as I began to pull myself back towards the edge.

Behind me, Mr Mumbles clawed up from below the murk. He shrieked an unholy shriek, filled with frustration and hatred and rage. The sound rebounded off the tiled walls. Round and round the room it went, growing gradually fainter with every rebound. Gritting my teeth against the pain, I heaved against the rope, and began to drift closer to the side of the pool.

My body was trembling too much to feel the fingers around my neck. The first I knew of them was when they forced me under. Down, down into the silent darkness of the water I went. The chill liquid wrapped around me, searching for some way in. I screwed up my eyes and clamped my lips together, denying the water its victory. For the moment, at least.

I turned sharply and felt the hands on my shoulders slip loose. Kicking hard, I shot for the surface, my lungs already on fire from the effort of keeping my breath in. As soon as my head cleared the water I opened my mouth, gulping in huge mouthfuls of air.

Twisting round I came face to face with Mr Mumbles. His hat was off – floating somewhere in the pool – and for the first time I saw him in all his horror. The thin, papery skin on his head was almost grey, and broken only by the occasional clump of thick, wiry hair. Each clump had been flattened by the wet, plastered down against his skull.

He looked grotesque. Diseased. Like a discoloured corpse brought back from the grave. I tried to swim away, but my stiff arms and heavy clothes made it impossible to move. It wouldn't have mattered, anyway. I couldn't swim a stroke.

With a short splash the smell of rotting meat was all around me once again, as Mr Mumbles moved in for the kill.

I lashed out, throwing slow-moving fists wildly in front of me, trying to drive him back. Each punch bounced harmlessly off him as he wrapped his hands around my throat for the final time.

There was no slow build-up this time. His fingers tightened instantly around my throat, almost crushing my windpipe. I tried to swallow down air, but his grip blocked the flow. Wildly I swung, hitting him as hard as I could on the head, the arms – anywhere I thought might hurt him. He didn't seem to feel a thing. We'd hit him with a car, and it hadn't hurt him. We'd smashed him into a wall. It hadn't hurt him.

If only I was stronger, like I'd been back in the garage with Ameena. If only I was strong enough to hurt him. The world rippled around me as my brain began to run out of oxygen. Limply I swung another punch. I don't even know if it hit the target.

Why wasn't I stronger? Why couldn't I fight him? I had beaten him when I was five, so why not now?

No time to figure it out. No time to do anything. No time left. No time.

My mind began to drift as the darkness closed in. Weird, random images flashed across it, like a slide-show presentation at a home for the criminally insane.

Click.

Mr Keller sticking a needle in a mutant child.

Click.

Nan screaming at me. *Where's Albert? Where's Albert?*

Click.

Mum in a tutu, twirling and spinning, around and around and around and around.

Click.

Me, floating in the pool – *this* pool – long ago. Motionless. Still. Arm bands tight on my arms. Like muscles. Big muscles. I am Superman. *I am the Hulk!*

The next punch caught Mr Mumbles under the chin and almost lifted him clear out of the water. He squealed as he flew backwards, falling just short of the edge. His head hit the corner of the tiled floor with a sickening *crack*.

In disbelief I stared down at my clenched fist. Had I really done that? For a brief moment I'd seen those blue and white sparks again, and felt an incredible sense of raw power pulsing through my body – even more than at the garage.

Now it was gone, and I was back to feeling nothing but the cold and the pain in my throat where Mr Mumbles' hands had been. But I'd hurt him. I'd become strong enough to hurt him because – just for a moment – I'd *believed* I was strong enough.

I looked down at the plastic bow wrapped around my wrist. The arrow had bounced harmlessly off him, but had I been surprised? Not really. I hadn't been surprised because I hadn't believed it would hurt him. That was where I'd gone wrong.

A low, mumbled groan drifted over the surface of the pool, as my friend-turned-foe righted himself in the water. We locked eyes, and for the first time I could see real pain in his. I saw blood begin to seep from his face, and for a moment I thought I'd done him serious damage.

Thick, dark, trickles of the stuff began to pour from the area around his lips. I gave a start, quickly realising the bleeding wasn't anything to do with me. Mr Mumbles was doing something he'd never done before. He was opening his mouth.

The first stitch tore through his top lip with a faint ripping sound. Soon another popped free, and another, and another, until the filthy pool was awash with red. I stared, unable to move, my gaze fixed on his eyes. Sunken eyes. Dead eyes. What was he doing? Why was he—

No! *Oh, no!*

With one final effort he tore open his mouth. Immediately, he began to retch, as if he was going to throw up. I turned and frantically tugged on the rope, dragging myself away from him – towards the edge, towards safety. It was no use, though. I was too late.

Behind me, Mr Mumbles roared in triumph, as gallon after gallon of filthy water spewed out of his mouth and down into the pool.

Chapter Seventeen

WATER WATER EVERYWHERE

The water hit the pool like a torrent, and was already rising fast. Everything was hidden below the scum-coated surface now: the doors, the windows, even Mr Mumbles himself. Still the water level kept moving upwards at an incredible rate, carrying me with it up towards the ceiling.

I yelped in shock as the rope which moored me to the wall went tight. Around me, the water continued to swell upwards past my chest. I barely had time for one big breath before the rising tide covered my head, and I once more found myself engulfed by a cold and bitter blackness.

My frozen fingers fiddled with the life ring, trying to force it off, but my clothes had become bloated in the water, and the plastic hoop was now wedged tight around me. No matter how hard I kicked and struggled, I couldn't get any higher; couldn't reach the precious, life-giving air just a few metres above.

A rush of panic washed over me as the dark depths brought vivid memories of the last time I was here flooding back. He had failed to kill me last time, but it looked like this time he was finishing the job.

I was drowning. My worst fear was about to be realised. I had seconds of air left in my lungs. The rope held me suspended in the cold, unable to move up. The swell of the water below made it impossible to move down. I hung there, suspended. Trapped. Dying.

A shape suddenly lurched at me from the dingy depths, and I kicked out weakly with my uninjured leg. A slender hand deflected the foot with ease, as a familiar figure swum into view.

Ameena gripped the plastic ring around my waist and tugged hard. She gestured wildly for me to help, and together we pushed and wrestled until, with one big, final heave, I was free. Clutching my arm, she swam up, kicking and pulling us through the water.

We hit the ceiling before we saw it. The water was all the way to the top of the room, and there was no surface for us to reach. Frantic with panic, we clawed at the crumbling plaster, desperately trying to find a way out. Ameena punched up at the ceiling, before recoiling in pain as her fist found the solid wood of the roof.

My instinct to breathe screamed at me, demanding I open my mouth, but I knew to do that would be certain death. Instead I peered up through the gaps in the plaster, searching for some way of escape. There had to be holes big enough to let in all the rain that had filled the pool. I knew there had to be one close by somewhere. I could almost picture it.

And suddenly there it was – a wide split in the roof just a little bigger than my fist. I reached my hand in, gripped the jagged edge, and pushed with every ounce of energy I had left. At first very little happened, but as I pushed, the timber began to bend in my grip. Almost. Almost there!

Snap! Even below the water we heard the wood break. The gap it left in the planks was just big enough for us to squeeze our heads through. We coughed and spluttered in unison as we filled our aching lungs.

'I t-thought it w-wasn't your f-fight,' I managed, my whole body shivering uncontrollably with cold.

'It's n-not,' Ameena trembled, 'b-but I thought m-maybe you could use a s-sidekick.' She tried to smile, but the cold wouldn't let her. Instead, she ducked down, making room for me to move. 'Now g-get out,' she stammered, just before her head disappeared below the surface.

It took several tries before my aching arms managed to drag me out of the water and on to the roof. The plastic bow slipped off my wrist and hit the roof with a faint clatter.

Shaking, I rolled over on to my back and watched the rain falling down on me. I was no longer able to feel it, my body already being soaked from head to toe.

With a splash Ameena's head popped back up from under the water. I rolled on to my side and reached a hand out to pull her up on to the roof. She batted it away playfully.

'Come on,' she snorted, 'j-just because it t-took you forever, doesn't me I can't d-do it first time. Watch.'

She bobbed down low, then leapt up, her hands pressed flat on the roof slates on either side, tendons standing clear of her forearms as she tried to pull herself up. Her upper body was almost clear of the water when she suddenly slipped back down.

'Ha!' I mocked. 'First t-time, eh?'

She looked up at me, her brow furrowing into a confused frown.

'N-no, I didn't slip, it's—'

The water burbled briefly as she was pulled down, mid-sentence. In the blink of an eye she was gone. I clambered on to my knees and shouted her name. The wind quickly whipped my words away, and carried them off into the storm.

Five seconds I stood there. No movement. I slipped the sodden school bag down off my shoulders. Seven seconds. I had to go back in. Ten seconds. I sucked in air and swung my legs down into the hole as I prepared to slip back into the water.

Ameena howled like a banshee as she pushed up,

sending me tumbling backwards on to the tiles. Throwing an arm out, I caught hold of hers. The water was pulling her down, making her heavy. A desperate roar of effort burst from my lips as I dragged her out on to the roof.

A second later, Mr Mumbles' face appeared at the hole. I slammed my foot down into it with as much force as I could muster, and enjoyed the crunch his hooked nose made beneath my shoe. As quickly as he'd appeared, my imaginary friend sunk back down into the darkness.

I knelt on the slates next to Ameena. She lay on her back, gulping and wheezing the life back into her body. She was trembling uncontrollably. We both were. If we didn't get dry soon we'd freeze to death.

Drained, I collapsed on to the roof next to her. We'd go in a second. Just a little time to get our breath back. Just a few seconds.

'You didn't save m-me there, by the way,' she stuttered. 'In case you thought you d-did.'

I could only look quizzically at her, unable to make my mouth form words.

'Y-you still owe m-me big t-time on the life-saving f-front,' she explained. Somehow, despite the pain and the cold, she managed a wide, toothy grin.

I smiled back at her. 'W-what else are s-sidekicks for?'

Fat droplets of rain tumbled from the heavens on to my face. I closed my eyes and let them wash over me, cleansing away the pool's filth. Maybe I'd have just a few seconds of sleep to recharge. Just a short nap to let my muscles rest.

A warning light marked 'Bad Idea' began to flash inside my head. I coughed and tried to sit up. It wasn't easy. My body was shutting down with the cold. Hypothermia was setting in. I had to get dry and warm. I forced my eyes open and rolled up on to my knees.

'Ameena,' I slurred, giving her a shake. She barely flinched and I noticed her eyes were also closed. I shook her again, more roughly this time. 'Ameena,' I shouted. 'We need to move!'

She groaned and opened her eyes. They swam wildly for a few seconds, before finally fixing on me. In an instant she was sitting bolt upright, scanning her surroundings, a puzzled look on her face. It took her a few more seconds to remember where she was.

'We have to get inside,' I told her. We used each other for support as we climbed shakily to our feet. 'If we don't get dry we'll die.'

'OK,' she nodded, no longer able to keep up the jokes. We joined hands and took a step towards the edge, leaning forwards into the wind in order to stay upright.

The moment we took that first step, a heavy *thud* shook the roof below us. We wobbled, caught off guard by the sudden shaking. A second *thud* sent a slate sliding off over the edge. It shattered on the moss-covered patio below.

'Oh, come *on*!' Ameena squealed. 'Give us a break!'

The tiles behind us leapt into the air at another *thud*. Faster and faster the bumping came, until with one final creaking and splitting of wood, a tightly bunched fist emerged up into the storm.

Ameena and I staggered and slid away until we were right at the edge of the roof. I risked a glance down at the ground below. It seemed a very long way away. My leg was still hurt from being twisted half out of its socket back at the house. There was no way I could make the jump.

But Ameena could.

'Go,' I told her. The sudden authority in my voice took me by surprise. Mr Mumbles was dragging himself through the hole he had made. His back was to us, but he'd be up and out in moments. He'd find us soon enough. 'Get down from here. Get away.'

'What?' she spluttered. 'What about you?'

'I can't make the jump. My leg won't take it.'

'I'm not leaving you alone with *him*!'

'I'll be fine,' I said. 'I've got a plan.'

'What are you going to do?'

My eyes fell on the bag I had abandoned over by the hole. 'I'm going to believe.' I turned to face her. 'But I need a few seconds to get set up.'

'So you could do with a *distraction*!' Ameena grinned. There was a sparkle behind her eyes – somewhere between excitement and hysteria. 'Why didn't you say? Distractions are my speciality.'

As Mr Mumbles hauled himself up through the roof, Ameena sprung forwards into a charge. Ducking low, she slammed her shoulder into the brute's back, before he even had a chance to turn round.

I watched Mr Mumbles twist and screech, trying to get a grip on the slippery slates of the roof. Ameena roared as she forced him onwards, closer and closer towards the roof's edge.

By the time they were nearing the drop, they were moving too fast to stop. Mr Mumbles plunged over first, with Ameena still gripping him tightly. I almost cheered. She wasn't just buying me time, she was using him to break her own fall!

I rushed to the edge and peered over. The rain battered my face, forcing me to narrow my eyes. It took me a few seconds to find the figures in the darkness, and when I finally spotted them, my blood ran cold as ice.

'No,' I muttered. 'Oh, *no*!'

Chapter Eighteen

FAITH

Ameena was face down on the ground, slowly dragging herself through the grass, trying to get away from the hulking shape of Mr Mumbles. He stood over her, watching her feeble attempt to escape. From the way she was moving it was obvious she was hurt – and hurt bad. Mr Mumbles, on the other hand, didn't seem to have been slowed in the slightest.

'Hey, baldy!' I shouted, as loudly as I could manage. 'How's that broken nose doing?'

He craned his neck and glared up at me. Even from this distance I could see the hatred burning in those dead eyes. 'You want me?' I yelled. 'Then come and get me!'

Ameena now forgotten, Mr Mumbles turned back to the

pool building. A rusted drainpipe ran all the way up to the roof. He took hold of it with both hands, his eyes still fixed on mine. Without a sound, he kicked his feet against the wall and began to climb.

He was fast for his size. *Too* fast. I had to move or he'd be on me before I was ready!

I hurried over to the bag, ripped it open, and thrust my hand inside. When I pulled it back out, I was clutching a handful of the plastic arrows. There were five of them in total. I hoped it would be enough.

No. I had to *know* they would be enough. I couldn't let doubt creep in. I had to believe the arrows would stop him, otherwise they – and I – didn't stand a chance.

My fingers shook as I pocketed four of the arrows and slid the notch of the fifth on to the bright yellow string of the toy bow. The whole thing felt frail and fragile between my fingers, like it would snap with the first pull. I prayed that it didn't as I took up my position at the very edge of the roof.

The wind buffeted me from side to side, but I stood my ground. I was sick of running, sick of hiding, sick of being afraid. This was the last stand, and if I was going to go out, I'd go out fighting.

Mr Mumbles was halfway up the side of the building now. He'd reach the roof in no time.

Unless I stopped him.

I gritted my teeth, pulled back on the bow, and fired.

TWANG! The arrow slipped from the string and was instantly carried off by the wind. Cursing myself I reached into my pocket and pulled out the remaining four. Clutching three of them between my teeth, I notched another and took aim.

TWANG! The arrow shot from the bow and curved off at almost ninety degrees, missing its target by several metres. I heard Mr Mumbles laugh as he pulled himself upwards.

TWANG! Another arrow whizzed away – closer this time, but still not close enough. I wasn't compensating properly for the wind. I slipped another notch against the string and aimed far off to the right of my target. I concentrated. There was only one arrow left after this. I had to make them count.

TWANG! A direct hit! The rubber suction cup bounced

harmlessly off Mr Mumbles' head, then floated off into the night. I lowered the bow. Why wasn't it working? I was using the arrows just like I had in the drawing, so why weren't they hurting him? What was different?

I took the last arrow in my hand and placed it in position. Mr Mumbles was almost on me now. One short burst of speed and he'd be here.

My mind raced back to that drawing. I closed my eyes and saw it clearly: every crayon mark, every detail. I could see the arrow embedded into Mr Mumbles' flesh. I could see the spray of crimson from his chest.

'Sorry, old friend,' I whispered. 'But this is *really* going to hurt.'

A familiar tingle crawled across my head and through my brain. I pulled back the string, opened my eyes, and let fly.

THWIP! The arrow cut through the air in the blink of an eye. For a fraction of a second I thought I saw metal glinting at the far end, before it disappeared deep into Mr Mumbles' shoulder.

His wail of agony split the night. The wounded arm lost its

grip on the drainpipe and he swung out from the wall. For a moment I was sure he was going to fall off, but no such luck. He wasn't finished yet.

Using just his feet and one hand, and with his face twisting in agony, Mr Mumbles continued his climb up to the roof. And I was all out of arrows.

My hand went into the bag again and brought out the toy sword. It was light and flimsy, but then so had the arrows been – to begin with, at least.

Giving the sword a couple of experimental swishes, I stepped back from the roof. Yet again, the storm battered me, as if the weather itself was my enemy. If only the wind would drop, even for just a minute or so.

Just a few seconds later, the wind did exactly that. Lucky. Lucky timing. Aside from the rattling of rain, the world was suddenly all but silent. It would make things easier. Not easy, but *easier*.

With a final growl, Mr Mumbles dragged himself up on to the roof and faced me. The arrow was still stuck in his shoulder, and as he got up I could see the rubber suction cup had somehow passed right through. It jutted out on the other side, thick with his oily blood.

We stood there watching each other for what felt like forever, neither one in a hurry to make the first move. My fingers gripped the sword handle tightly. The plastic buckled in my hand and I felt all confidence drain away. I was facing a monster, and I was armed with a child's toy. I had just begun to wonder what it would be like to die, when Mr Mumbles did something unexpected.

He spoke.

'Conngraaatulaaaationnnsss,' he said. His voice was a low hiss – unsteady, like he was testing it out for the first time. 'No one belieeeved you'd lassst thisss long. You've ssssurprised usss all.'

'Who?' I asked, more than happy to stall for time at this point. 'Who have I surprised?'

A low, sickening cackle escaped his blood-crusted lips. 'You didn't think I wasss the only one, did you? I am just the firssst,' he sneered. 'There are thousandsss of us, hidden down there in the Darkesssst Corners. *Millions*. And we're coming back.' His eyes lit up with crazed delight. 'You thought you could jusssst *forget* about me. But I'm coming back! We're all coming back!' He gestured around with his good arm, not once shifting his gaze from me. 'And then all this – this entire worthlessss world – will burn. We'll destroy it all!'

The Darkest Corners. Those three words almost sent me staggering backwards off the roof. But that had all been a dream, hadn't it?

It didn't matter now. If I lived through this, *then* I could worry about the Darkest Corners. Right now, nothing mattered but stopping the monstrosity standing before me.

'No, you won't,' I said. My voice was calm and steady – the exact opposite of how I felt inside. I couldn't let him see my fear. I had to keep bluffing. 'That's not going to happen.'

'Oh, reeeally? And who's going to ssstop us?' That cackle again, like a hyena's death rattle.

With a flick of my wrist I held the sword out. The blunted point aimed right between his dead man's eyes. 'Me,' I declared. 'Just me.'

And with that, I lunged.

Chapter Nineteen

A FIGHT TO THE DEATH

I'd never fenced before, so there was no skill in any of my movements. Even if the blade had been razor-sharp metal, Mr Mumbles would still have managed to deflect it away just as easily as he did.

On my second or third swing with the sword, he dodged to the side, sending me off balance. I stumbled and almost slipped on the sodden grey slate of the roof. It took just a moment for me to find my centre of gravity again, but he was behind me now, laughing. Always laughing.

I swung the sword round in a sweeping arc and spun on my heels. Mr Mumbles leaned backwards and easily avoided the blow. Once again I overstretched and teetered forwards, my balance lost. My hand steadied me against the slates, and I was up again.

Every move I made he was ready for. He dodged and weaved, effortlessly avoiding my every blow. The wind was beginning to pick up again, and even though the sword weighed next to nothing, I could feel my arm growing heavy.

'You will never beat meee,' he sneered, ducking to avoid another flailing swing. 'You think you can huuurt me, but really you have no idea.'

'That arrow seemed to do the trick,' I reminded him. To hammer the point home I leapt forward and managed to whack the exposed end of the arrow with the tip of the sword. He roared in pain and retreated back two or three paces.

'A lucky ssshot,' he growled.

We began circling each other, only the flimsy plastic blade of my weapon between us.

'I beat you once before.'

'And yet heeere I am.'

'Not for long!' I cried. With a roar I leapt at him, sword raised above my head. It whistled through the air as I swung it down at him. A second before it connected, his fingers wrapped around my wrist.

'You don't get it, dooo yooou?' he cackled. A blurred shape hit me in the face like a freight train and the world turned shades of grey. The fist came up again. I didn't see it move; didn't feel the sword slip from my fingers; didn't notice the blood on my chin.

Mr Mumbles' bloated lips were moving, but I could hear nothing over the sound of crashing water. It filled my head and the world around me, drowning out all other noise. Except that laugh. Throughout it all I could still hear that laugh.

The third punch caught me on the side of the head. I was flat on the roof before I felt it. The world flickered, then the pain in my jaw dragged me back from the brink of unconsciousness.

'How do you think I came to exist in the firssst place?' Mr Mumbles demanded. He was bending down, his face close to mine. Despite the torrent in my ears, it was impossible not to hear him from such a short distance. 'You brought me into the world. You and your slurred sssspeech and your crying and your need for a friend, *any* friend – you *made* meee.'

My chin touched against my chest as he hauled my head up. *Crack!* He slammed it back down on to the slate, and I felt my whole skull vibrate.

'You maaade me and then, when you didn't need me, you cast me out. You sent meee away and then you forgot me! Did you reeeally think I was going to let you dooo that?'

My lips moved of their own accord, but no sound emerged.

'We were supposed to be friendsss,' he shrieked. 'And you sssend me away? You sssend me to *that place*? Have you any idea what I've been through? The thingsss they did to me? *Look* at me! *Look what they did!*'

I didn't respond. Nothing I could say could stop him doing whatever he was about to do. He was a madman, beyond reason. I felt a sudden weight on my chest as he pressed a knee against it.

'Beg meee,' he snarled. 'Beg me for your life and I might keep you alive as my sssslave.' His grotesque mouth stretched into an unpleasant grin. 'For old times' sssake.'

'P-please,' I managed. The movement made something in my jaw grind painfully together. 'Have a breath mint.'

His face fell before I'd even finished the sentence. Shrieking like a demon he hit me again. *Bang!* An ear exploded in pain. I stretched my arms out and flailed them around me, searching for the sword. Nowhere to be found. *Bang!* Another blow, across my cheek this time.

Nan's words suddenly swam before my eyes. They burned, bold and bright, lighting up the night. My imagination was strong enough to create Mr Mumbles, so my imagination was strong enough to send him away. The arrow had worked because I'd believed it would work. No, not believed – because I had *known* without even the faintest shadow of doubt that it would work.

The light bulb. The axe. The shield. Even the exploding donkey. It really was me. All of it. It had all happened because I'd wanted it enough. No, not *wanted* it, because I'd *imagined* it.

Mr Mumbles was on me now, the weight of his body

pinning me down. His fingers crawled through my hair and I yelped as he took hold. Grinning in triumph, he lifted my head and slammed it hard against the slates once again. Something at the base of my skull felt as if it were about to shatter. If only I could reach the sword. If only I could find a weapon.

Suddenly I remembered something I'd slipped into my pocket at the police station. I wrenched my wrist around and fumbled for it, struggling against the weight of my imagined attacker.

As he hit me again I found what I was looking for and yanked it from my pocket, already feeling the electrical tingle across my scalp.

This had to work. It was *going* to work. I knew it. I knew it without the faintest shadow of a doubt.

I pressed the water pistol against Mr Mumbles' stomach. He looked down at it, then back up at me. His laughter rang even louder in my ears. He was speaking to me, shouting something. I couldn't hear him. I didn't care.

My finger squeezed on the trigger. With a deafening roar

the water pistol spat flaming hot lead into Mr Mumbles' belly.

The impact of the bullet lifted him off me. He flailed backwards, then hit the slates with a wet thud. Traces of smoke curled up from the water pistol as I watched him convulsing, his hands clutching at the wound in his gut. One thing was for sure: he wasn't laughing any more.

Despite the hole in his stomach, it didn't take him long to recover. He was back on his feet before I reached mine, but he was more cautious this time, and didn't dive straight for me.

The water pistol was useless now. It was tiny, and even *my* imagination couldn't picture it holding any more than one bullet. It dropped at my feet with a metallic clatter.

'Impressssive,' Mr Mumbles conceded. He threw out his arms and hurled himself at me. 'But not impressssive enough!'

I rolled across the roof and caught the blade of the toy sword between two fingers. Still plastic. Good, I needed it light.

With a final effort I turned and hurled the sword. The effort sent me tumbling backwards to the tiles, but my aim was good. End over end the sword went, and as it spun it began to change. The dull grey plastic took on the shiny sheen of steel. The safe, rounded point became sharp and deadly. In less than two seconds it had changed from a play thing to a lethal weapon, hurtling directly towards Mr Mumbles' head.

He easily snatched the sword from the sky, somehow managing to catch it by the handle before the final spin could cut his head in half.

'Stupid boy,' he growled. He took a step towards me and raised the blade above his head. 'You missssed me.'

'Maybe,' I shrugged. I felt an electric tingle creep across my entire body this time. The hairs on my arms stood up straight, as I imagined the most destructive weapon I possibly could. 'But maybe not.'

I looked up – the storm was moving away from the village now, but I could see lightning sparking from the clouds on the horizon. Could I do it? Was it even possible?

That doubt again. I pushed it away.

I would *make it* possible.

With a fluorescent *crack*, a bolt of lightning stabbed down from the sky. The jagged streak of blue struck the tip of the sword, and for a moment the world went a blinding white. I threw up my arms, shielding my eyes from the brilliant explosion of light.

When the flash had faded, I looked across to where Mr Mumbles had been. Now there was nothing, save for a small pile of ash and a plastic sword, warped and melted and black. As I watched, the wind swept up the dust, and carried it off to be swallowed by the swirling night.

He was gone. I'd done it. The nightmare was over.

I couldn't get his words out of my head, though. He said there'd be more of them. Thousands of them. Maybe *millions*.

I shuddered at the thought. If the Darkest Corners was real, then those things I'd seen in it had to be real, too, and if they somehow made it through…

But no. The Darkest Corners had been a dream. The most vivid, detailed dream I'd ever had, yes, but a dream all the same. It was done. Finished. Mr Mumbles was gone.

Finally!

'Did I miss the excitement?'

I turned in time to see Ameena pulling herself up on to the roof. It was a struggle for her, but she made it.

'Yeah,' I winced. Pain pulsed through my head, down my spine, and on to any other part of my body it could find. 'Some sidekick you turned out to be.'

Her face went pale as she saw the blood and bruising on mine. 'Good grief,' she gasped, 'what did he do to you?'

'It looks worse than it feels,' I said. 'No, wait, I got that the wrong way round.'

She gave me that Cheshire Cat grin and half guided, half dragged me back into a standing position.

'What about you?' I asked.

'I'll live,' she replied. 'It only hurts when I'm conscious.'

I decided there and then that it was time for the truth. We'd been through too much tonight to play games any longer.

'Your family didn't really buy the Keller House, did they?' I asked. She opened her mouth to argue, then decided against it.

'Don't have much in the way of a family,' she told me with a shrug. 'Just me. Still thought I might crash here, though. For a little while, at least.'

I nodded, unsure what I should say. In the end I decided on: 'The pool could do with a clean.'

'Thanks,' she smiled. 'I'll bear that in mind. Now come on. Let's get you down.'

Chapter Twenty

NOT THE END

Mum was awake and lying on the couch when Ameena and I stumbled into the living room, each holding the other up. The side of Mum's face was a dark purple. It bulged weirdly in places it shouldn't be bulging at all, but she was alive, and that was all that mattered.

'Kyle!' Nan yelped, her frail hands flying to her mouth at the very sight of me.

'It's OK, Nan, I'm OK,' I said, trying to reassure her. 'It's over.'

'Did you... is he gone?'

'He's gone,' I nodded. 'He's gone.'

Mum tried to sit up, but the movement must've hurt and she slipped back down again almost at once.

'*Mum*,' I said, the relief obvious in my voice. 'You're OK!'

'Fine,' she nodded, attempting a smile. 'But you – look at you. Was he, I mean, did he... ?'

'I'm fine,' I assured her. 'A new head might be nice, but other than that I'm perfect.'

She smiled again – for real this time – then closed her eyes.

'How is she?' I whispered, turning to Nan. 'Really?'

'She's fine,' promised Nan, who was holding up surprisingly well, all things considered. 'She just needs some rest, is all.'

I sagged down into an armchair and let my head roll backwards. 'I know the feeling.'

Nan shuffled up behind the chair and loomed over me. From this position she looked like she was upside down. Upside down, and worried.

'Kyle,' she said, 'we didn't know. How could we know? We thought... we didn't...'

'It's OK, Nan,' I nodded. 'I'd started to doubt it all myself, and I'd been the one it was happening to. You couldn't know.'

She nodded, briefly, and glanced away. When she looked back, her eyes were wet with tears. 'I'm just glad you're all right,' she said, her voice hoarse and raw. I felt her arm slip on to my shoulder. I took it in mine and gave it a squeeze.

'You too,' I replied. 'Oh, and by the way, nice work with the vase.'

We laughed at that, and she gave my hair a playful ruffle. I didn't have the heart to tell her it was agonisingly painful.

'Oh, I found this pinned to the door,' she said. She held out a large white envelope, which I slowly took from her. The contents were rigid. A card? I looked at the writing on the front. My name, but the handwriting was unfamiliar. I glanced across at Ameena, who had taken a seat on one of the dining chairs. She gave a shrug.

'I dunno. Open it.'

I wasn't sure why, but my hands shook as I tore along the top of the envelope. Maybe I expected a trick of some kind – some fatal, final farewell from Mr Mumbles.

All I found was a Christmas card. It was silver and red

and covered with glitter all the colours of the rainbow. In bright, bold letters on the front were the words: 'Season's Greetings!'

Still half expecting danger, I carefully eased the card open. A rectangle of shiny paper slipped out on to my lap. I picked it up. The temperature in the room seemed to drop as I examined the photograph in my hand.

'Is this... is this some kind of joke?' I demanded. The question was addressed to no one in particular.

'What is it?' asked Mum, opening her eyes.

'It just appeared on the door,' Nan answered. 'I don't know, someone must have come in and left it there when I wasn't looking.'

My heart thudded all the way up into my throat. The picture showed me in my bedroom – or an impression of it, at least. But half the room wasn't my bedroom at all. A line cut the picture in half from top to bottom. On the right side was my room, with me standing in it.

The left-hand side was completely different. The peeling wallpaper was grey and shabby, the carpet threadbare and worn. It looked exactly like the corridor the man in the Darkest Corners had led me down.

So that place *was* real. I'd been there. This proved it.

I frowned, looking down at the photograph. When was it taken? Why was the image split in two? It was almost as if...

Mum managed to stand up. She shuffled over to me and took the picture from my trembling hands. I heard her gasp, before she staggered and fell back on to the couch. Her eyes were wide, staring, and fixed on the picture.

'Mum?'

'This is your *room*, Kyle,' she sobbed. 'What... when was *he* here? When was he in your room?'

'Who?' I asked. But I knew. I already knew.

'*Him!*' she wailed, holding the photo up for me to see. She pointed at the empty space next to me. 'Your father! When did you meet your father?'

I'd known the words were coming, but they still somehow came as a shock. My eyes flicked down to the Christmas card I held in my hands. There, inside, scrawled in handwriting even more untidy than mine, were four short words. I breathed deeply as I read them over and over again: *It begins*, they said. *Love, Dad.*

I folded the card closed and crossed to the door. Mum was still talking, but I could no longer hear her. The storm whistled and whispered at me as I peered into its heart. There was no one in sight. Whoever had left the card was long gone.

It begins. What did it mean? I had no idea, but as I turned and pushed closed the door behind me, I had a horrible sinking feeling I would find out soon.

I just didn't realise *how* soon.

Still here?
You really want more terror?

Or is it just that you're too afraid
to turn the light off, and
you're hoping these last pages might
contain some nice, comforting words?

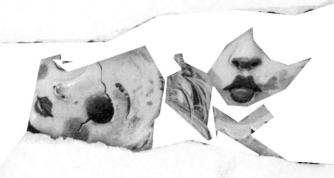

Well, they don't. But if you do want more chills,

then feel free to read on for a sneak peek at

the blood-curdling action in the second

INVISIBLE FIENDS book, *Raggy Maggie*...

I was in the school canteen. I was tied to a chair, and the bruising on my face hurt like hell.

I looked around at the room. It was bright and clean. Daylight shone through the windows. As I studied my surroundings, I noticed my chair was now positioned right next to one of the canteen's big round dining tables. Small, floral-patterned cups and saucers had been laid out in three places – one in front of me, one directly across the table, and the third halfway between those two. Another chair had been positioned at the placing across from me, but not at the one on my right.

A sugar bowl and a milk jug sat on the table too. Like the cups, both of these were empty.

From over my left shoulder I heard a whimper. By craning my neck as far as it would go, I could make out the shape of someone lying on the floor.

Mrs Milton was curled up into a ball, her knees almost to her chest, her arms clutching her head. Her whole body was shaking. Every few seconds it would twitch wildly, forcing another whimper from her trembling lips.

'Mrs Milton?' I said. Although I spoke softly, the sound still made my skull throb. She didn't respond, so I tried again. 'Mrs Milton, are you OK?'

'She doesn't want to play with us any more.'

I froze. The voice was the same one the headmistress had used – or maybe *it* had been using *her* – but it hadn't come out of her mouth. It had come from somewhere further behind me, beyond my line of sight.

I recognised the voice right away as the one I'd heard during my first visit to the Darkest Corners.

'Caddie.'

The little girl in the dirty white dress stepped into my line of sight. 'Oh, you remembered,' she beamed. As she did, the bright line of lipstick across her mouth curved into an exaggerated smile, like the grin of some demented clown.

'What did you do to her?' I demanded.

Caddie's face fell. Her wide, dark eyes blinked rapidly, as if fighting back tears. 'She won't play any more,' she said. 'We were having so much fun, but then she just wouldn't play.'

Down on my left, the headmistress gave another low sob. 'S'not fair,' Caddie sulked. 'Every time I find a new friend to play with they get broken.'

I twisted in my seat and looked down at Mrs Milton. She was rocking back and forth, weeping, shaking – a shadow of the woman she had been. Bruised. Battered.

Broken.

When I turned back, Caddie was standing by the table. Her back was to me and she was fiddling with something on the tabletop. The way she was bending her body made it impossible for me to see what.

'Where's Billy?' I asked.

'Not telling.'

'What have you done with him?'

'I told you, silly,' she giggled, turning back to face me. 'I'm not telling!'

She skipped past and disappeared behind me, leaving me alone with the thing she'd been positioning on the table.

The porcelain face of the doll was slumped sideways on the bundle of grubby material that made up its body. A long dark crack ran from the top of its head and down the left side of its face, completely obscuring one eye. The other eye squinted across the table at me, painted on, but eerily lifelike.

Raggy Maggie had seemed disturbing enough in the Darkest Corners, but here in the school the doll was somehow even more chilling.

'Tea?'

I jumped in my seat as Caddie appeared beside me. She was holding a small plastic teapot. Her wide eyes looked at me, expectantly.

'What?' I spluttered. 'No.'

Immediately her face darkened, as if a shadow had crawled across it. 'But it's a tea party,' she glowered. 'Why would you come to a tea party if you weren't going to have tea?'

I glanced from Caddie to the doll on the table. Its single eye bored into me, as if waiting for my answer.

'Go on then,' I croaked, turning back to the little girl. Her face brightened at once. 'Just a small one.'

'Oh, goody,' she trilled. 'Maybe if you're *extra* good you might even get a cake.'

I nodded nervously. 'Yum.'

Maybe you're wondering why I was so scared of a girl with a doll. If so then you've obviously never met Caddie. If you had, you'd know *exactly* why I was playing along with her little tea party scene.

As soon as I'd set eyes on her in the Darkest Corners, I could tell there was something 'wrong' about Caddie. At first glance she looked more or less like any other five-year-old girl, but it didn't take long to realise she was something much more sinister than that.

Partly it was her eyes – the irises almost filled them, so dark as to be virtually black, like two gaping holes in her head. The make-up didn't help, either: dark blue circles ringing the eyes, a crimson smear across the lips, and a smudge of red on each pale cheek.

The words she said could have been those of any other kid her age, but the way she spoke implied a deeper, darker meaning behind them that only she was aware of. She also had a strange intensity about her, as if she were three wrong words away from becoming very, very angry. Somehow I knew that making her very, very angry would be a very, very stupid thing to do.

Caddie was, in short, more frightening than any little girl had any right to be. And as for the doll... Don't get me started on the doll.

Caddie hummed below her breath as she tipped the spout of her teapot over my cup. Nothing came out, but this didn't seem to bother her in the slightest.

'Sugar?' she asked, when she'd finished pouring.

'No,' I said. 'Thanks.'

She frowned briefly, but said nothing, and carried on round the table to where Raggy Maggie was slumped. Once again she tipped the contents of her toy teapot into the waiting cup. 'Raggy Maggie likes sugar, don't you, Raggy Maggie?'

The doll, as expected, didn't reply.

After spooning some invisible sugar and pouring some imaginary milk into her doll's cup, Caddie moved around to the opposite side of the table and took her seat. She was so short she had to stretch up in the chair to pour her own pretend tea. Milk. Eight sugars.

'Drink up,' she giggled. She took a sip from her own cup. The *shlurp* sound she made was surprisingly convincing. 'Oh, I forgot,' she said, smiling, 'you can't. You're all tied up.'

'What do you want?' I asked.

Shlurp. 'Mmm, a biscuit would be nice. A chocolate one. With sprinkles.'

'No, I mean... *what do you want?*'

She sat her cup down on the saucer. Those dark, empty eyes of hers fixed firmly on me. I could feel the doll staring at me too, but I tried not to think about it.

'Just to play,' she said with an exaggerated shrug. 'We just want to have fun, that's all. Nothing's fun where we live.'

'The Darkest Corners.'

Her face changed in an instant. Her eyes narrowed, pushed down by her eyebrows as her mouth pulled into an angry snarl. 'Don't you say that,' she cried. 'Don't say that place!'

She was on her feet before I knew it, snatching up her cup. She thrust it sharply forwards, as if throwing her imaginary tea. I almost smiled, before the pain hit me.

Nothing had been poured into the cup, and I saw nothing come out of it, but as soon as she'd chucked it towards me a blisteringly hot liquid hit the top of my school jumper and began to soak through my shirt.

I let out a hiss of shock as the skin on my chest began to burn. Caddie continued to glare. I knew she wasn't going to help me. No one was. I had no choice but to screw my eyes shut, grit my teeth and wait for the pain to pass.

The worst of it probably faded in less than a minute,

although it felt like longer. In just a few minutes more I was left with merely a dull ache, although it was made worse by the fact my shirt was clinging to it.

Caddie was still standing up on the other side of the table, but her face was no longer twisted so fiercely. She gave a little cough as she lowered herself back into her seat and poured another cup of boiling hot nothing.

'That was your fault,' she explained. Her voice was back to normal again, all trace of the rage that had gripped her gone. 'I didn't want to do that, but you made...'

Her voice trailed off and she turned to look at her doll. 'What's that, Raggy Maggie?' she asked, reaching over and carefully lifting the bundle of rags off the table.

She held the doll to her ear, moving its head up and down slightly, as if it was whispering to her. For a moment I almost wondered what it was saying, until I reminded myself it was only a toy.

'Hmm, I don't know, Raggy Maggie,' Caddie murmured. Her eyes were still on me, not blinking. 'You think we should do *what* to him?'

I watched the scene playing out before me, barely aware that I was holding my breath. My hands wriggled at my back as I struggled to free them from the rope or wire or whatever it was that was holding them together.

It was no use. The harder I struggled, the deeper my bonds dug into my wrists. All I could do was sit there. Sit there and wait to find out what Caddie had in store.

'Oh, but he's a *nice* boy,' Caddie protested. 'He might be our friend.' The doll's head waggled up and down more forcefully. 'He didn't know they were bad words,' the girl continued. 'It's not fair!'

Raggy Maggie stopped moving – just for a moment – then gave a final few nods of her head.

'OK,' Caddie nodded, her face brightening. She turned her wrist so the doll's solitary eye was looking towards me. 'Raggy Maggie wants you to say sorry for saying the bad words,' the girl explained. 'I think you'd better. She's very cross.'

My lips had gone dry. I licked them, but there was no saliva left in my mouth, so it didn't help. 'Sorry,' I croaked.

'Say it properly.' Caddie stood up and stretched across the table, holding out the doll so its expressionless face was just a few centimetres from my own. Up close it smelled sour, like a carton of milk a month past its sell-by-date.

'Sorry for saying the bad words,' I said. I felt like an idiot, but more than anything I wanted the doll out of my face.

'Thank you for being so nice, Raggy Maggie,' prompted Caddie.

I hesitated, but then carried on. 'Thanks for being so nice.'

Raggy Maggie's porcelain head bobbed up and down. As it did, Caddie spoke in a harsh, scratchy voice. 'You're welcome,' the voice said. 'Don't do it again.'

The doll was pulled back across the table, but wasn't put down in its place. Instead Caddie held on to it, both of them facing me. We sat there in silence for a long time, the occasional whimper from Mrs Milton the only sound to be heard.

I was about to say something – anything – when Caddie spoke. 'We're going to play a game,' she told me, her eyes sparkling with excitement. My heart sank. The groans from the headmistress testified to the damage Caddie's games could do.

'What kind of game?'

'A *fun* game. It's like hide and seek, only *better*!' She was bouncing up and down in her seat now, barely containing her delight. 'Me and Raggy Maggie will go and hide somewhere, and you've got to find us.'

'OK...' I said, hardly believing my luck. Once they were out of the way I could find a way to get free and escape. 'Sounds good.'

'I'm not finished yet, silly,' Caddie giggled. 'Because we're not going to be hiding all by ourselves. We're going to be hiding with our best friend in the whole wide world.' She hugged Raggy Maggie tightly to her face. 'Billy.'

That complicated things a bit, but not much. I would still go and get help. Yes, Billy might be stuck with Little Miss Crazy and her dolly for a while, but he'd made my life a misery for years, and I found it difficult to feel too bad for him.

'And here's the best part of all,' Caddie gushed. 'We'll all be hiding somewhere here in the school, and if you don't find us in one hour...' She glanced at her doll and giggled. 'Billy *dies*.'

From *Raggy Maggie.*

Available July 2010 from Harpercollins *Children's Books.*